WE VOW IN SIN
SINNERS' PLAYGROUND

M.T. MORGAN

Copyright © 2023 by M.T. Morgan

All rights reserved. No part of this publication may be reproduced, distributed, or transmitted in any form or by any means, including photocopying, recording, or other electronic or mechanical methods, without the prior written permission of the publisher, except in the case of brief quotations embodied in critical reviews and certain other non-commercial uses permitted by copyright law. This book is a work of fiction. Any resemblance to actual persons, things, living or dead, locales or events is entirely coincidental.

We Vow in Sin

Editor: *Rumi Khan*

Cover Designer: *Melissa Cunningham, To All the Books I Love*

Photographer: *Wander Aguiar*

TO MY FAVORITES.
CAMILLE, AMANDA, KEEANA, KIRA, NICHOLE, AND DANIELLE.
THANK YOU ALL FOR BEING SUCH AN AMAZING SUPPORT SYSTEM!

WARNING

This book contains subject matters some may find triggering.
This story includes:
Molestation
Bondage
Abuse
Murder
Violence
Rape
Dub-con
Due to that, this story is not for everyone. Please take that into consideration before reading this book. You will not be comfortable in all aspects of We Vow in Sin.

National Sexual Assault Hotline

1-800-656-4673

INTRODUCTION

DEAR READER,

THE SINNERS' PLAYGROUND SERIES IS MEANT TO BE READ IN ORDER, STARTING WITH *WE DANCE IN SIN*. IF YOU DO NOT START WITH BOOK ONE OR CHOOSE TO GO BACK AND READ IT, PARTS OF BOOK TWO MAY NOT MAKE SENSE AND/OR RUIN THE SHOCKING TWIST I HAVE IN STORE FOR YOU. *WE VOW IN SIN* TAKES PLACE AS SOON AS *WE DANCE IN SIN* ENDS.

MOREOVER, THE NEXT PAGE CONTAINS A LIST OF POSSIBLE TRIGGERS IN THIS BOOK. IF YOU CHOOSE TO AVOID SPOILERS, I TOTALLY UNDERSTAND. I TRUST YOU TO KNOW YOUR OWN MIND AND TRIGGERS.

XOXO,
　MT

PLAYLIST

Unstoppable- Sia
Send the Pain Below- Chevelle
Pray- Jessie Murph
Dark Paradise- Lana Del Rey
I Am Machine- Three Days Grace
Bad Liar- Selena Gomez
Demons- Imagine Dragons
Chasing Pavements- Adele
Silence- Marshmello ft. Khalid
Sweater Weather- The Neighbourhood
Gangsta's Paradise- Coolio
Someone You Loved- Lewis Capaldi
Summertime Sadness- Lana Del Rey
Man in the Box- Alice in Chains
Everlong- Foo Fighters
Happy Song- Bring Me the Horizon
Replay- Zendaya
The Search- NF
Sink into Me- Taking Back Sunday

Loser- Beck
Sail- Awolnation
Unsteady- X Ambassadors

PROLOGUE

PRIMROSE

I've lived my life in a cage. Like a zoo attraction everyone comes to admire.

Coming here, this isolated college tucked into the forest, is the freest I've ever been. I get to wake up when I want to, go to bed when I want. Wear what I want. There is no schedule, telling me when to eat, when to get dressed. Nothing. It's up to me to take care of myself. Find trouble on my own.

And I found it.

The crisp wind makes the small flyways around my face shift as I sew a button on a dress. That's what I do. I make clothes. My favorite is ball gowns. Momma got me a sewing machine when I was small. She understood about having clipped wings. Father loves to collect pretty things, leaving them in a glass box to be admired. Only bringing them out to show, never to love. Momma told me to create something beautiful, to express myself through my art. When she handed me a sewing machine and a book on the art, she freed me. If only for a couple of hours a day.

My fingers work smoothly and quickly as I sit under the tree outside The Misfits' home. The Misfits—I had no clue what I was getting into when I caught the eye of the mafia prince. My only objective at the time was to take control of my own life. Find my own freedom. But Vance... He wasn't really in my cards.

The man that's so feared, no one dares to make eye contact with him, is gentle with me. His words are soft, eyes burning hot every time he looks at me. As if I'm the one weakness he can afford in life. Unfortunately, he is not a weakness I can have. No matter how much I want to. Things between us have been tense since I've paraded other men in front of him. To push him away. And since I took a bullet for Brixley, everything has been wrong.

I don't regret it, how could I? I may have a scar, but she could have lost her life.

My hand flies to the nasty scar on my face at the memory, turning my mood sour. It doesn't matter, though, because I need to pack soon. Summer break is two days from now, and Momma, she's not good. Breast cancer, stage four. They didn't catch it in time. It's spread everywhere in her body, making treatment not an option. Instead of going with Brixley this summer, I'm going home. Somewhere I promised myself and Momma that if I ever escaped, I'd never return. But someone has to take care of her. I'm all she's got. And if I were dying, I'd want someone to hold my hand, so I know I'm not alone.

Walking into the house, I take the stairs up to my room. Closing the door quietly, I rip the cap from my head. Sighing as I brace myself on the vanity. *Look up, Primrose. Embrace your new appearance.* My hands shake as I slowly raise my face to the mirror. It's like an out-of-body experience. As if I'm watching myself from behind my shoulder. My crystal blues freeze over, tiny drops of salty liquid dripping down the curve of my cheek, dripping over the scar. A large, tan hand cupping my chin, pulling my soul back into my body. His touch is gentle, warm as he cradles my face, pulling my head toward his strong chin. My eyes shut as our bodies connect, a warm, electrical current sparking deep inside of me. "Tell me what you need." His voice is a deep whisper against the shell of my ear. "I think you're perfect, but if you want it gone, I'll make it happen, Angel. Just say the word."

It would be so easy to give in. To fall prey to the beast behind me, allow him to fix everything for me. To the outside world, we seem like more, but between us, nothing has ever happened. Sure, there is some flirting, maybe some stalkerish tendencies, but we've never been anything but platonic. He was my mentor, my guide into this world. My protector as I made my way through the trials, but that's all it's ever been. Or that's what I tell myself. Because I can't trade one cage for another, and with what our future together would look like, that's exactly what it would be.

"I don't want or need anything from you," I whisper.

His grip tightens on my chin. "You remind yourself that tonight when you wake up screaming, wishing I was there to hold you in my arms as you fall back to sleep," he growls, releasing me. I stumble into the vanity, my hands placed on the edge as I refuse to look into the mirror.

The lies we tell each other will be our downfall, I just know it.

VANCE

I jerk into a sitting position, sweat dripping down my body as I listen to the sharp cries no one else seems to hear in this house. My legs move before I do, making my way to her room. I quietly close the door, sliding into her bed until our bodies are connected. I take her trembling body into my arms, laying a soft kiss to the tip of her head. "You said you wouldn't come," she hiccups.

I don't respond. For the last few months, Primrose has actively tried to push me away. And I won't lie and say it hasn't worked. As possessive as I feel of her, I can't get over the fact that she would give herself to another. Since I first laid eyes on her, I haven't so much as looked at someone else. I've seen that guy leave her room, heard them laugh as I paced my own, trying to convince myself not to make his body disappear. No matter what, though, I can't stop caring. And that makes her a weakness. *I don't have room for weaknesses.* I should have never allowed her in my life, because now, she's in it forever. No matter what, The Misfits are for life. "Be quiet," I say, no heat behind my words.

We stay in silence for a long moment before she speaks again. "Will you drive me home?"

It takes me by surprise. I thought she would be with us this summer, but maybe going home is what she needs. To be somewhere safe, somewhere familiar. "Yeah, Angel. I'll take you home."

Her body grows limp in mine, her breaths evening out like they always do when she falls asleep. Carefully, I leave her bed, going back to my own. Staring at the ceiling, I convince myself that time away from one another is exactly what we need to get over these feelings we have for each other.

I just have to shut it all down. I'm Vance fucking Da Luca, mafia prince. I don't have feelings. Or that's what I tell myself.

I STAND WITH BECKETT AGAINST THE WALL OUTSIDE PRIMROSE'S room. "How is she doing?" he asks softly.

I shake my head. "It's been seven months since that night and she barely leaves her room, and when she does, she wears a cap low over her eyes, trying to hide her face. The bullet skimmed her cheek, but it's permanently scarred." I sigh, running my hands over my face. "I'm taking her home for summer break. Maybe her being somewhere she's comfortable will help her. Fuck knows I can't." And I think that's the part that kills me the most. I couldn't protect her and now I can't help her.

Beckett pats my shoulder and I jerk away from him. Not wanting his pity or his touch. "What we went through is traumatic—for anyone. But for someone as sheltered as Primrose... it's going to do some lasting damage."

Yeah, Devlin's journal was filled with psychotic writing. Outlining every murder. Wish I could kill that fucker again. "I know, but she's so ashamed of her face now. I offered to have a plastic surgeon come in, even though I don't think there is a single aspect of Primrose Thatcher that isn't perfect. She refused. And fuck," I sigh, again. I'm not sure why she refuses my help all the time. As if we haven't been close this entire year. As if I'm not the one chasing her demons away.

Primrose's door opens and I smile. "You ready to go, Angel? It's..." My words trail off as a guy walks out behind her. "Who the fuck is that?" I demand.

She pulls the bill of her hat down, shielding her face from us. "He's a friend. He lives close to me so he's just giving me a ride home," she speaks quietly.

Something inside me fucking snaps. "Sure. Just a friend." I storm past her, slamming my door.

Fuck this.

WATCHING PRIMROSE LEAVE WITH THAT GUY WAS ALL I NEEDED TO close it all off. It's been a few weeks since she left me in the hallway, refusing to allow me to take her home. It stung, but eventually, it went away. Like every other feeling I've ever had.

Beckett and Brixley sit in my living room with me. My sister rattling on about her new engagement ring. Telling me about color schemes I couldn't give two fucks about. My phone dings and as I look down, my face splits into a grin.

"Why are you smiling?" Brixley asks.

Looking up to my sister, I smirk. "Because I just arranged my marriage."

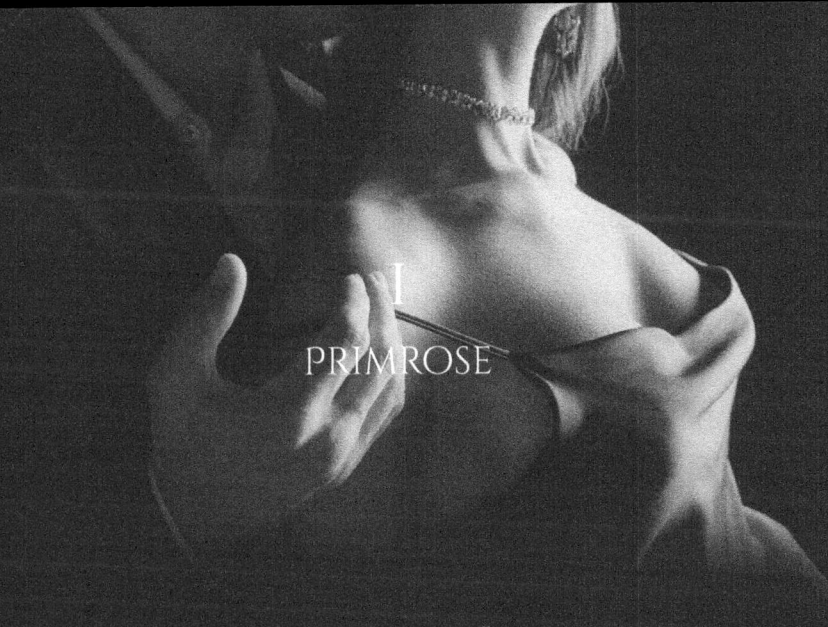

I
PRIMROSE

"Time of death, three forty-two p.m."

I stare straight ahead at the deep maroon walls. Momma loves maroon, she scattered the color anywhere she could. My hand squeezes tightly around her warm, fragile hand. I feel nothing. I expected to be screaming in rage, crying in desperation. But truly, I feel numb. So numb, I wonder if this is all a dream.

My head shifts on the pillow, lifeless eyes stare back at me. Momma's eyes. She never closed them as she died. She rattled against the last struggles of her life all while staring at me. Through me. When I came to check on her, I heard the noise. A gurgling, yellow wet liquid foaming from her mouth. I called for Daddy; he didn't come. He was off somewhere, probably with Momma's replacement. I had to roll her body. She wasn't heavy but I'm not strong, so it took time, and then finally, with Momma on her side, the noise wasn't as bad.

I called an ambulance even though Daddy forbade it. Still, they didn't get here in time. I crawled on the bed as Momma's sickly pale body shook, her eyes wide and rolling as if looking at something not in this world. I brushed wet hair from her forehead, begging her not to leave me just yet, but she did. And now I lay here, in bed with Momma. Hand still tightly holding on to her stiff one.

"What is going on?" I don't even turn to look at him. My father. "Primrose, I asked you a question."

"She's gone." The voice that leaves me is not my own. It's hard and cold, emotionally drained.

"Then get up and let them do their job," he lashes out. My hand tightens on Momma's. "Now, Primrose."

"No."

"Excuse me?" His voice is closer now, his hand latching onto my arm. And not for the first time, his grip is far too tight.

"I said no," I state firmly. *Brixley and Amiyah would be proud.* I shake his grip off of me, refusing to look at him.

His hands grab onto my shoulders, and something inside me snaps. I scream. My body wrapping around Momma's as Daddy tries to tug me off of her. "Let go, Primrose," he roars.

I struggle against him, my hands digging into Momma's nightgown. I watch as it tears beneath my fingers as I'm wrenched away from her body. My legs kick out, my screams of desperation and sorrow echo in the room until my body is slammed against the wall. And then it's all silent.

Father fixes his suit jacket, combing his hair back with his fingers. "Now, go fix the thing on your face. We have company in an hour."

And then he is gone, but I can't move. Not when they load her up, placing a sheet over her body. The EMT looks at me sadly as he wheels her out. The maids come in, sweeping her scent from this earth as they change the bedsheets.

Almost as if she was never here.

I LIKED IT BETTER WHEN MY SCARS WERE ON THE INSIDE, OR WHEN they could be hidden behind a scrap of clothing. Not this long, jagged, disgusting pink thing on my face. My finger brushes over it, my stomach lurching with the need to puke. I rarely look in the mirror anymore. Not that I've ever been overconfident in my looks, but at least my face didn't make me want to vomit. And according to my father, my looks are my greatest asset.

I move on autopilot, brushing liquid foundation over the imprint left from his bruising grip on my arm. At this point, I'm an expert. He never cares if people can see, whisper about the horrors of this house, but I do. Momma's eyes flash in my mind, a single tear rolling over the curve of my scar. I don't stop it from dripping from my chin, splashing onto the black material of my dress. Leaving a path through the freshly painted foundation.

I paint heavy globs over the scar, but it doesn't even begin to hide the new flaw on my face. The ugliness of it reflecting my insides.

Tarnished.

Ugly.

Broken.

I set the makeup sponge down, picking up the tube of mascara and coating my lashes. *This will have to do.* My face is swollen, puffy, and dead. No amount of makeup can hide the red splotches on my cheeks, the lack of life in my eyes, or the scar on my face.

A dinner party. Momma died two hours ago. And he wants to have a dinner party? My father is a cruel man, covering up the darkness by going to church. A man of God, he proclaims. If there is a God, I can assure you, he does not look after my father. And he doesn't support my father's version of repenting my sins. I shake my head, the memories of that alone will send me over, and I'm barely hanging on as it is.

I chance a glance in the mirror, quickly moving my hair to hide my scar from view. *He said he'd fix it for you*, the voice in my mind reminds me. But that's just it, I don't want anything from *him*.

I make my way out of my room, walking down the hall of clean and wholesome. The cream walls covered in scripture and family photos. The white carpet without stains. There's never been any fun in this house. The carpets were not hard to keep clean.

As I step down the stairs, I hear light chatter, the clanking of utensils as they eat. I am an hour late, but I don't care. I deserved a minute to gather myself. Keeping my face cast down, I walk to my chair, quietly taking a seat. My plate waits in front of me, but I can't stomach anything. My mind flashes back to Momma's cold dead eyes. My brain starting to separate as I shake silently in my chair. I can only hear static as the memory of finding her choking in bed makes my fingers curl around the arms of the chair. How bad would my father punish me if I just left? If I stood and ran to my room, if I hid in the closet, knees to my chest as I screamed?

"Primrose." Like a lash, my father's voice whips across me.

Say something, darling. Don't make it worse on yourself. I can hear Momma's voice whisper next to my ear. As if she is gone but hasn't quite moved on just yet. "Yes, Father?"

Can I even call him that? He'd never been a father. Fathers love their little girls, and mine, well, he punished me instead.

"Greet our guests." His voice is clipped and chilled. Not a warning, a promise.

I tilt my chin up slightly, my eyes still cast down at the food I won't be touching. "Hello," I say. My voice is raw and raspy. "I hope your evening is treating you well?"

I couldn't care less how their evening is going, but I have to pretend. Pretend as if my mother didn't just die in my arms only hours ago.

"So, this is the infamous daughter?" a man says.

My father chuckles and it makes my insides twist. "Yes, this is Primrose Thatcher."

"The one with the gunshot scar?" I do flinch visibly this time, my hand going to my cheek. Heat blooms behind my touch, embarrassment and shame washing over me as I look to my lap.

"Unfortunately." My father chuckles nervously. "But she's still... well..."

"Beautiful." *That* voice stops me in my tracks, my eyes sweeping up and locking with *his*. Time stops as we stare at one another. His eyes fill with a fire that scorches every inch of my face. *Vance De Luca.*

"So, you'll still take her?" my father asks hopefully.

Take me? What?

Vance rubs his bottom lip, never breaking eye contact with me. "You would rather sell your daughter to the De Luca Devil than pay your debt?"

My eyes fly over to my father, my heart beating harder,

faster. It's not as if I didn't know this day wouldn't come. Since I was a small child, I was told my marriage would be arranged. Momma said it's more common than one would believe. But I honestly couldn't understand it. My family has ties to the mafia. The De Luca one. Not directly Vance's, but his uncle. My father is a contractor. Making bodies disappear under someone's future home is a no-brainer.

"Why, yes. As you can see, she's not much use to me with that thing on her face now." I flinch a little at his words. Father has always praised me on my beauty, how some man would pay him handsomely someday for my hand, but since the incident, he can barely look at me.

Vance's fist curls on the knife in his left hand, jaw ticking. "Very well. We have a deal, Mr. Thatcher." Vance then snaps at the man next to him. He doesn't look much older than me. Maybe his eyes do, which are clouded with something dark. "Get the papers."

I rise before I know what I'm doing. The chair crashing hard behind me. My father glares at me. "Down, now, Primrose."

I shake my head, backing away. "No," I whisper. It's not a rejection to the marriage, it's just too much to take in, in one day. Plus, father said we would wait until my *pointless studies* were done. It seems as if he can't wait to get rid of me.

My father rises, his hand going up, and I flinch away from him. "Touch her and you lose your hand. The only one laying a finger on my future wife will be me," Vance says patiently.

My eyes flick open as I watch my father. He won't touch me now, but later—the promise is there. I take off, running up the stairs and shutting myself in my room. My heart beating fast as I sink in front of my bed. A scream bubbles up in my throat and I release it. Screaming at the top of my lungs as I bang against the floor. I don't know how long I stay there before my eyes grow heavy and I slip into unconsciousness.

I WAKE TO SOMETHING NUDGING MY SHOULDER. I BLINK MY EYES open, taking in Vance. He wears black slacks, his shirt unbuttoned a little at the top, exposing the glorious, deep richness of his tattooed skin. His heavy arms rest against his sides as his hands hide deep in his pockets. His head tilts, causing the coal black of his hair to fall in front of one of his eyes. "Angel," he rasps.

Before tonight, that last time I saw Vance, he was storming away from me as I declined his offer to give me a ride home from college. I want to say it wasn't personal, but it was. Vance and I, we have this strange relationship. Not as friends, but not more either. We lie somewhere in the gray matter on the black-and-white scale. My first year of college was full of his sinful face. Most of the time, hidden by a bandana. Because of him, I am now a member of The Misfits.

A relationship that started off with teasing and flirting soon turned cold as I began to talk to someone else. It was never serious, but he never gave me a chance to explain that. Lust turned to hate in the span of a school year. And now, here we are. Me on the floor curled up at his feet.

He bends at his knees, dropping to his haunches as he pulls a black velvet box from his pocket. My eyes snap shut. Today is too much, too fast. I feel his callused finger on my face, on the broken scar that shatters my image. The touch somehow stings even though I know that's impossible. I flinch away from him, my eyes opening slowly.

Vance's face hardens, his sharp jaw molded from stone, ticking. His nostrils flaring, causing the light to catch on the diamond stud there. He drops the velvet box next to my face. Getting to his feet slowly, he never loses eye contact with me.

"I'll be back for you soon." He looks around my room as Samson, my cat, jumps up on my bed, meowing for Vance's attention. Vance grabs my traitorous cat. Samson purring loudly into his black dress shirt. "Pack your things, Primrose."

He stalks away, but I find my voice. "Vance." He pauses, looking over his broad shoulder at me, still petting my cat in his arms. "Please, don't do this," I whisper.

"It's done, Angel." And then, he's gone.

It takes some time to pull my weak, aching body up from the floor. I take a shower, hoping the ruins of today will disappear down the drain with the soapsuds. After dressing, I sit at the foot of my bed on the floor. My legs folded under me, as I rest my hands in my lap. My forehead is pressed to the mattress as I wait. My door opens, the eerie quiet is like a ticking bomb as my door shuts gently. I don't hear his footsteps, but I feel him. His dark, looming energy that is the same but so different from Vance's. "Repent, Primrose."

I don't tense as I hear the leather of the whip he smacks against his hand. "Disobedience," I say as the first slap cuts across my flesh through the silk material of my night shirt. I bite my lip to keep from screaming, it'll only give him more pleasure. "Embarrassment." The next whip is harder, cutting a slit into my skin through my shirt. The cool air of the room stinging the mutilated flesh. I continue ticking off my flaws, the ways I've failed my father and our God. With each confession, a sharper, harder lash against my skin.

"Do not forget ugly," Father whispers. Clutching my hair in his fist and throwing me to the ground. The hit lands on the sensitive flesh of my side and I muffle a groan into the carpet. "Don't forget to pray for your sins, *daughter*," he sneers, but then breaks off into a chuckle. "Although, the Lord can't even save you from your doom of marrying the De Luca Devil. Fitting, isn't it? I guess you'll finally pay for all your sins."

I lay on the floor of my room, not for the first time today, but it would be the last.

2
VANCE

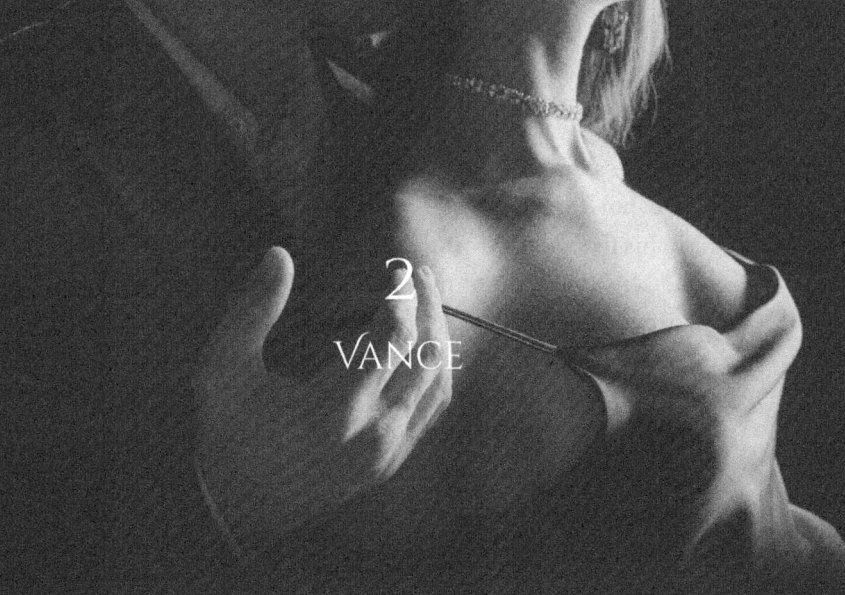

ADRIANO, my cousin, side-eyes me as I sit outside the Thatcher house. Watching her window, and not for the first time. *Primrose Adonna Thatcher.* The girl who's been plaguing my every thought for almost a year now. Her father borrowed money before I knew anything about her. But as fate would have it, she showed up on my campus, radiating light that drew to my darkness instantly. Her father is scum, and I, the bastard that I am, took the situation in my own hands and molded it to my liking. I knew he'd give her to me. No matter the nightmares that are whispered about my name, the cold bloody life of the Italian mafia. Her father simply does not care as long as he gets what he wants. In this case, to be rid of his debt and his daughter. He was surprised I would want her, considered her as damaged goods now. The world is pathetic if it can't see the beauty that radiates from her.

"If you want to say something, cousin, say it," I grit out, watching my angel's light finally flicker off. I haven't left since dinner. After watching her father raise a hand to her, a hand he almost lost and was going to choke on, I knew I could not leave her here another night.

"Are you sure you want to do this? We have excellent candidates lined up if you want to get married."

I didn't want to get married, but fate, the evil bitch, laid the perfect opportunity in my lap. "Positive, cousin."

"But her face," Adriano says innocently. Innocence will get you killed in our world.

"Do you like your tongue?" I ask.

Adriano pauses, swallowing hard. "Yeah."

"Utter one more word that disrespects my future wife and you won't have one."

Adriano nods. "Okay, I get it."

Good. Soon the world would get it, because Primrose is mine. You don't touch, look, or disrespect what is mine.

Samson jumps in my lap from the back seat, purring and rubbing his silky fur on me. Meowing as if telling me to go save his savior. "Patience, Samson. We must wait."

And we do, until around three in the morning. The devil's hour. And then, I go after her.

I PEEK DOWN AT HER LAYING FORM FROM ABOVE MY BANDANA. She's so small in the lavender bed, only taking up a small portion of the king-size mattress. I let my eyes drift over her succulent body, feasting on the milky thighs that show due to her kicking the covers off in her sleep. When I used to watch her, before Devlin happened, she dreamed peacefully, but tonight, nightmares plague her, shown by the small frown of her lips, the way her eyelids are creased and not smooth.

I should feel like an asshole for what I'm about to do, but I don't. Because my angel deserves this after she gave what's mine to someone else. I grit my teeth, slowly lowering my body over hers so she's pinned down. Her eyes flash open, and I grin. She can't see it, though. Her body thrashes, her lips parting in a scream, but I place the duct tape over her mouth to silence her. The way the black material flashes off her dewy skin makes me hard. Grabbing her wrists, I bind them together. Rolling the tape around them up to her elbows. It's not tight, but she still can't escape me. She bucks under me, trying to roll from beneath me, but it's futile. I ease off of her, grabbing her ankles and wrapping the tape up to her knees.

Grinning, I drop the tape to the floor. Admiring my handiwork. Bound, broken, and beautiful. I don't look at her face. I know if she's crying, I'll snap. Instead, I hoist her small body over my shoulder and carry her down the stairs. Once I reach the car, I pound on the trunk. I brought one of my flashy babies out for the occasion tonight. Adriano pops the trunk open and I drop my angel in like a sack of potatoes, not giving her a second glance as I shut the door.

"You need serious help," Adriano mumbles beside me as I throw the car into drive.

"Truer words have never been spoken, cousin."

LIQUID FIRE. HER BLUE GEMS LOOK LIKE TWIN BLUE FLAMES AS I gently lay her body down in the spare bedroom across from mine. I didn't think the sweet creature in front of me could possess such hatred, but here it is, focused straight on me. I can't blame her, can I? For being so mad. I basically kidnapped her in the middle of the night. Sure, I could have not bound her in duct tape before throwing her in the trunk, but where is the fun in that?

I pull the knife from my pocket, gliding it gently along her foot as her body scoots to the edge of the bed. Her toes are cold, slightly pink. The lack of circulation taking its toll on her. Careful not to nick her, I cut the duct tape away from her legs, watching as her small toes wiggle with freedom. Next, I cut the tape from her delicate arms, unraveling the tape from her milky flesh. She stretches her arms, fists curling slightly as her eyes shoot daggers at me. My lip tilts as I wonder if maybe she'll throw those little fists at me. I wish she would. I deserve it. With far less gentle fingers than I've used on her, I rip the tape from her mouth. She doesn't make a sound, just continues to stare me down.

"That wasn't necessary," she finally says, pushing herself up into a sitting position.

"No," I say, rubbing my bottom lip, "but it was so much fun." There is something different about my angel. As if she could have possibly broken more since the last time I saw her. Her crystal eyes resemble shattered glass as she looks up at me.

She cuts my thought short when she says, "Now, if you could please leave, I'd like to sleep. And honestly, I deserve that much after the little stunt you just pulled."

She's right, of course. She deserves a little peace from me. With a nod of my head, I turn. Heading for the door and shutting it quietly behind me.

I don't sleep. Not with the creature that runs marathons in my mind under the same roof as me. Instead, I get up early, watching the sunrise as I drink my coffee on my back deck, inhaling my first cigarette of the day. The birds chirp quietly as the trees sway. The breeze only a little crisp, smelling of summer. The light pale blues of the early morning, hinting at rain. I'm thinking of how peaceful it is, when I hear my front door slam. Looking over my shoulder at the open back door, I see my pain in the ass walking briskly toward me. Her shadow closely behind.

"That was fast," I mumble, taking a drag and blowing thick smoke into the air.

Brixley, my fierce little sister, comes barreling toward me. "Are you fucking crazy?" she asks, red hair wild from sleep. Ninety percent sure those are pajama pants she's wearing.

"My therapist likes to call it *misunderstood*."

She smacks my arm. "You can't force people to marry you."

I look over to Beckett, my best friend, the traitor. "I asked for twenty-four hours."

He shrugs. "She got worried, couldn't get a hold of Primrose. You know I don't like to see her upset."

Pussy-whipped and so unashamed of it. Bastard. I sigh, "Soulless, it's seven o'clock in the morning. This could have waited."

Her doe green eyes narrow. "No, it couldn't. Primrose's mother died yesterday."

That gives me pause. I know every detail of every situation I'm entering, but somehow, this huge factor was left out, overlooked. Her dad sure as fuck didn't act as if he just lost his wife last night. I take another hit of my smoke.

Maybe this is why my angel looked more tarnished than usual. "She didn't tell me."

Brixley throws her hands up. "Why would she? From my understanding, you forced your way into her safe space and demanded a marriage."

"Not quite, but close."

"Where is she?" Brixley demands.

"Guest room." I nod toward the stairs.

She's gone without a backward glance, racing through the house. "Fucked up this time." Beckett smirks.

Maybe he is right, but I feel as if I'm finally doing everything right.

3
PRIMROSE

I wake to a mess of red hair falling over my face. A small body curled with mine. *Brixley.*

A small smile tugs my lips as I gently push the copper mess from my face. Brixley mumbles something in her sleep and I giggle, just slightly. Green eyes pop open to look at me just as the door swings open, Amiyah pushing her way into the room. "Bitches are napping without me."

Amiyah smiles, diving onto the bed next to me. "I'm so sorry, love," she says, curling around the other side of me until I'm squished between the two. My back protests in pain, but I ignore it. For the first time, I feel safe. My body trembles as emotions rush over me, clouding my mind in pain and grief.

"Shh," Brix says, wiping salty liquid from my eyes. "It's not okay, but we will get through this together."

I shift and my back aches. The tears stream harder, the bout of ugly crying coming with no end in sight. "I'm breaking," I choke out.

It feels as if I am drowning in cold misery. Numb with frostbite on the tip of my heart. Mind muddy with black tar.

So thick I can't see past the darkness. "It's a lot. It's so much, but you got this. Vance will take care of you, you know?" Brixley continues to swipe my tears away.

"I'm trading one cage for another," I hiccup.

"Being a mafia wife is so badass, though. Imagine the power, the fear," Amiyah says, and I crack a tiny smile.

"The marriage is the smallest part of my misery. I just lost my mom and everyone is acting as if she was never here."

They both grow quiet before Brixley asks, "When is the funeral?"

"Tomorrow."

"We will be there. To support you," Amiyah says, holding me tight.

"But right now, let's get you cleaned up, yeah?" Brixley suggests, rising from the bed. She walks to the adjoining bathroom of my new room in Vance's house, and I hear the water run.

My friends are very well aware of how shy I am. Thankfully, they don't know the truth as to why that is. They leave, giving me space as I slip into the scolding water of the bath, watching steam rise. It feels impossible to wrap my mind around the last twenty-four hours. And if I'm honest, I don't want to. I want to live in this numb bliss, suppress the onslaught of emotions that will eventually boil to the surface, spilling through the top like lava. But right now, I'm so exhausted. I don't even want to try. I let my eyes close, my head tilting back against the black tile of the wall. Sleeping with my nightmares were impossible last night. But right now, my mind is so blank, I drift into a sleepless void of nothing.

THERE IS NO NOISE, NOT A SIGNIFICANT THING THAT WAKES ME, but my eyes flash open. Allowing me to see the dark orbs of the devil staring back at me. He leans against the counter, ankles crossed, arms braced behind him. My body jerks in the lukewarm water as I pull my knees to my chest, trying to hide myself from his view. He tsks. "Come on, Primrose. I've seen you countless times."

My nose scrunches up. "Excuse me? When?"

Vance smirks, his eyes blazing as he says, "You had a nasty habit of leaving the curtains open when you changed at the dorms."

I shake my head, I knew he had stalker tendencies, but I didn't understand how deep they ran until just now. "That's an invasion of privacy."

Vance shrugs, grabbing a folded fluffy towel—black, of course—from the cabinet next to the dark marble sink. "Doesn't matter now. Come on, get out." He opens the towel for me, gesturing me out.

I shake my head. "Not until you leave."

Vance's eyes narrow as he takes a step closer to the bathtub. "Get out or I'll make you. It's up to you."

I bite my lip. I don't want him to see the wounds on my back. If I keep my back to him, maybe I can avoid it. Or maybe, he won't care. I was only his initiation, maybe since that is over he will no longer feel the need to protect me. Sighing, I step out of the bath, my cheeks turning a rosy shade of pink as I look to the ground. Water clings to my body, and the bathroom tile beneath my feet is a warm blessing to my chilled body. I reach for the towel, but Vance is quick, turning my body fast, my back slamming into his chest, but the towel doesn't wrap around me.

The air is tense, and I feel a pressure push down on my chest as we both stand in silence. "Angel, I'm going to ask you a question." Vance's voice is just above a harsh breath.

"Okay."

"And I don't want you to lie to me."

I pause, waiting for a beat. "I'll try not to." It's the best I can offer.

"Who did this to you?" His finger lightly brushes down my spine.

I close my eyes, something akin to shame wrapping a noose around my neck as I try to think of a lie. A lie to protect a man who has never protected me. "I... I can't think of a proper lie, and honestly, I don't have the energy for this. Can you please just give me the towel?"

"I see," Vance says lowly, wrapping the towel around my body and leading me to my room. He sits me in front of the vanity, his strong hands wrapping around the handle of the brush. With gentle strokes, he brushes my hair. I don't look up from my firm stare on my lap. I'm sure if I wasn't so trapped in my mind, I would love this, but as it seems, I'm going to be stuck in the cage inside my mind for a while. "Primrose," Vance says softly.

"What?" I whisper.

"Why didn't you tell me about your mom?"

I humorless laugh spills from my lips. "Should I have done that before or after you duct-taped me and put me in your trunk?"

His hand freezes around the brush. It falls to the ground as his hand twists inside my hair, jerking my head up so I'm looking at him through the mirror. "A simple text would have worked. We used to be close, or have you forgotten the entire past year?"

"Oh, you mean how you were always in my business? Or how about the cold shoulder you've given me since the incident?"

He pauses, eyes narrowing. "I made it perfectly clear I never wanted to be your little fucking friend and, yet, you had the audacity to have that boy over at the house. Give him what belongs to me," he spits.

It clicks, he thinks I slept with Cooper, which is what I wanted him to believe. I can't really blame him, can I? "Who I *fuck* is none of your business."

He jerks on my hair, causing pain to explode around my scalp. A mean grin lights up the dark depths of his eyes. "That's not true anymore, is it, *fiancée*?"

"Vance..." my voice chokes out, and I fight back tears. "I can't do this right now. So, either be supportive or get out. You wanted me and now you have me, at least have the decency to allow me to mourn my mother," I snap.

He sighs deeply. "All right. Go lay on the bed so I can clean your wounds before they get infected."

Brixley chooses that moment to be my savior, "No worries, I got her."

Vance glares at his sister. "Soulless, I thought you left."

"You wish, Satan. Now, move. I think you've done enough." She bats his hand away from my hair. I watch them stare each other down until Vance finally breaks. Brixley is the only person walking this earth who could make him back down.

"Now," Brixley smiles at me, "tell me who did this to your back or I'll make Vance look like a saint."

After another stare down, this one featuring me, I finally tell her.

The sky is a deep gray and purple, a beautiful contrast as it openly weeps. Rain slides against my umbrella, dropping to the freshly dug dirt at my feet. Momma always loved the rain, it's like a small sign from her. Amiyah pulls me into her side as she lays her head on my shoulder. Brixley is on my other, lightly sniffing on my behalf. I watch our lifelong preacher as he talks about Momma. How she will be missed but she's in her forever home now, along with my baby brother. We lost him to SIDS at only a month old. I was six at the time, and I remember that's when my life really began to change. When Momma and Father started to fight, when I had to start repenting. Father always wanted a son, and that was his last chance because Momma refused to have another child, claiming it could never replace the son she lost.

A warm touch on the small of my back jerks me to the here and now and I realize tears are freely flowing, slicing down my face. "For you are dust, and to dust you shall return."

A small whimper escapes me as my body shakes with unshed grief. Like a dam, I break open, wishing I could go to the safe place of numbness. My whimpers turn into loud uncontrollable sobs as people place handfuls of dirt on my momma's casket. My body is jerked back into a strong, sculpted chest, and I nuzzle my face inside Vance's jacket.

"Get a hold of her, she's embarrassing me," my father hisses.

I feel Vance's body go stiff. "Watch your mouth, Mr. Thatcher, before I cut your fucking tongue out. I'll treat my fiancée as I please." He pauses, before continuing, "In fact, you'll be coming over tomorrow. You and I have some business to discuss. And you'll have Primrose's room packed and delivered to her new home as well."

I don't have to see my father to know he is glaring but nodding. Somehow, I quiet myself, seal my emotions enough to let go of Vance. He looks down at me, nodding at whatever he sees in my eyes. With trembling hands, I kiss my rose as I look down at the dirt people have already tossed on top of her. I missed my queue to place my rose, but I refuse to leave until I get the chance. "Your battle is over," I whisper against the rose. "You're finally free, Momma." I drop the rose, before walking to Amiyah's car.

4
VANCE

A<small>DRIANO PALES</small> at the knife I'm sharpening in my shed. I personally hate the sound, but the fear of watching Mr. Thatcher slowly lose his shit is refreshing. If he pisses himself, even better. "Do you think cutting up your future father-in-law is the best idea?" Adriano asks.

"Fuck if I care." I shrug, turning to face my *future father-in-law*. "Now, what did I say about touching my fiancée? Oh," I grin, "that's right. No one but me will lay a hand on her and yet," I drop to my knees in front of him, "you did just that." I look over my shoulder to Beckett, who stares down at his phone. He usually isn't here, but he asked—nicely, might I add—if he could watch. "Beck, you want to hold his wrist or feed him his fingers?"

Beckett shoves his phone into his pants pocket. "Neither, really. Is there a third option?"

I grin. "Hands, it is."

Beckett stretches Primrose's sperm donor's hands out in front of him. As someone who will take the throne one day, getting my hands dirty is not something I usually get to do, but I didn't ask, and this is personal. "Are you a vegan?" I ask Mr. Thatcher. He pales, shaking his head slowly. "Good. Good. Into cannibalism by any chance?" No response. "I'll take that as a no. That's very unfortunate for you. But hey," I shrug, "who knows? Maybe you'll enjoy this so much you'll thank me someday." He whimpers, but thankfully he knows begging will get him nowhere, as he's dealt with my uncle many times.

Beckett snickers and Adriano comes up beside me. "I'm feeding him his fingers, huh?"

"Look at you, more than just a pretty face." I raise my hand and bring my knife down on his pinkie. Blood squirts across my shirt, getting in Beckett's hair. Beckett usually gets hard at the sight, but this time he glares. "*Bon appétit*," I say just as my future father-in-law chokes on his pinkie.

I SIGH AS I WALK INTO MY HOUSE. SPYING THE LITTLE REDHEADED pain in my ass sitting on my couch, eating my fucking Oreos. "Why are you still here, Soulless? Go the fuck home already." Brixley narrows her eyes at me, tossing an Oreo in her mouth. "And stealing from the mafia will get you killed."

She snorts, putting my fucking cookies down. "I just... Prim is so sad and honestly, I don't want to leave her here alone."

"I'm here."

She makes a face. "Not that I'm not rooting for you two, but you have shit timing as well as manners."

I sigh, pulling my phone out, "I think you and that shithead boyfriend of yours are probably playing some sort of fucked-up game. Not that you don't care for Primrose, but I have this hunch Beckett doesn't know where you are and your phone is off." I raise my eyebrows at her.

Brixley sighs. "Fine. He's just been a little overbearing."

I shrug. "I told you to stay away from boys, you didn't listen."

"Please don't tell him."

I grin. "Too late, you have about five minutes to get the fuck out before he shows up."

"You're a horrible brother." She stands, grabbing her things and my fucking Oreos, before heading for the door. *Little shit.*

I find Primrose in the guest room she is staying in, unpacking boxes. She has on a thick sweater, long, white-blonde hair braided and cascading down her back. The first time I saw her, I thought I was hallucinating. She was this light, beautiful creature that made the campus look dull in comparison. Her round face and high cheekbones. The soft pink petals of her lips. The arctic eyes surrounded by thick, black lashes. Small, almost translucent freckles dotting under her eyes and over the bridge of her nose. She was so bright and innocent, sometimes it physically hurt to look at her. I knew I had to have her.

I lean against the doorframe, watching as she takes out fabrics and lays them next to a sewing machine. I've watched her countless times as she's made dresses and clothes. Her clothes have always looked so deep and rich. Imagine my surprise when I realized she was the one who made them.

Primrose gasps when she spins around and sees me. "I really don't want to see you right now." She always speaks her mind. I can't exactly tell if she's just naïve or stupid.

"I know you're mad, but here's the thing, Angel. It was

me or someone else. Your father has been looking for suitors for months."

"So, the devil I know is better?" She shakes her head. "This is the twenty-first century, I shouldn't have to worry about this."

"No, you shouldn't, but that's not your reality." I move across the threshold, invading her space even more than I have. She pulls out an old garment bag, laying it gently on the bed. "What's that?" I ask.

She pets the old material inside, a tear dropping down her cheek. "My mother's wedding dress."

I swallow. I'm not great when it comes to my emotions or dealing with others'. They always make me uncomfortable. "Will you wear it?"

"Parts of it. I plan to add pieces to mine." She turns to me. "Which reminds me, when will we be getting married?"

"Soon."

She pursers her lips. "Then I'll need to begin making my dress." She pulls her phone from her side table. "Am I free to leave or is this a prison?"

I grind my teeth. "You're free until you give me a reason to lock you up."

"Great. Then I'm going with the girls to buy more fabric." She flips her braid over her shoulder. Focusing on her phone as her fingers fly across the screen.

"I would like to have dinner tonight, together. We'll go out somewhere nice. Get out of the house."

She frowns. "I... I don't like going out in public," she whispers.

"Why is that?" I ask, stepping closer to her.

"People like to stare."

"That's because you are a beautiful sight."

She laughs humorlessly. "No, Vance, it's because I have this nasty scar on my face."

I'm not blind. I see the scar, but to me, it only enhances the beauty that she is. I'm just not sure why she and the world don't see what I see. I press my front to her back, watching as her breathing becomes faster as I cup her chin, turning her face to mine. I lower my face to hers. My lips brushing hers as I say, "There is nothing wrong with your face." I trail my tongue from the corner of her lip, dragging it over the scar. She shudders in my arms, eyes closing.

"I just need more time. I'm not ready to face the outside world just yet, okay?"

I nudge my nose against hers. "Okay. I'll order in." It takes a tremendous amount of strength to pull myself from her. I don't want to let her go, but even I know her life has been shifted upside down. I walk out of the room and into my home office. Adriano waits for me, lounging on the couch. "I want you to follow her," I say, sitting at my desk.

"Like a bodyguard? Why?"

I pull a cigarette out, pushing it between my lips as I light it. "Because," I say around my cancer stick. "After this year, I'll be taking over the family business. That's not news to anyone, which puts my future wife in danger."

Adriano nods. "I know in order for you to take over, you have to get married, but why her, exactly?"

I pause, my free hand twitching on the gun under my desk. "Why not?"

"She's so... weak. You need someone strong to be able to handle the role as your wife."

I blow smoke into the air, trying to contain the anger I feel toward my cousin. "Ever been shot in the face, Adriano?" He shakes his head. "Very well." I pull the gun from its holder, the barrel aiming at his face. "If I shoot you in the face, what do you think will happen? Will you cry like a little bitch? Maybe die? Would you hide from the world?"

Adriano pales, shaking slightly. "I don't know."

"Correct." I cock the gun. "That's the difference. Primrose does know and just look at her, still standing tall, finishing her degree, making a fucking wedding dress as we speak. You don't need to understand why I chose her. Just know her pinkie has more strength than your entire persona. Now get the fuck out of my office."

As soon as Adriano is finally out of my sight, I exhale, putting the gun away and clicking my computer awake. I watch Primrose as she finishes up neatly unpacking her life. I watch as she pulls the sweater from her body, her lush curves making my cock stiffen. She puts her back to the mirror, peeking over her shoulder to inspect the welts and slashes her father left behind on her dewy skin. I should have killed that fucker. Should have, but I didn't because I wasn't sure how Primrose would take that. And she's been through enough.

And yet, she will still have to pay for giving away what's mine.

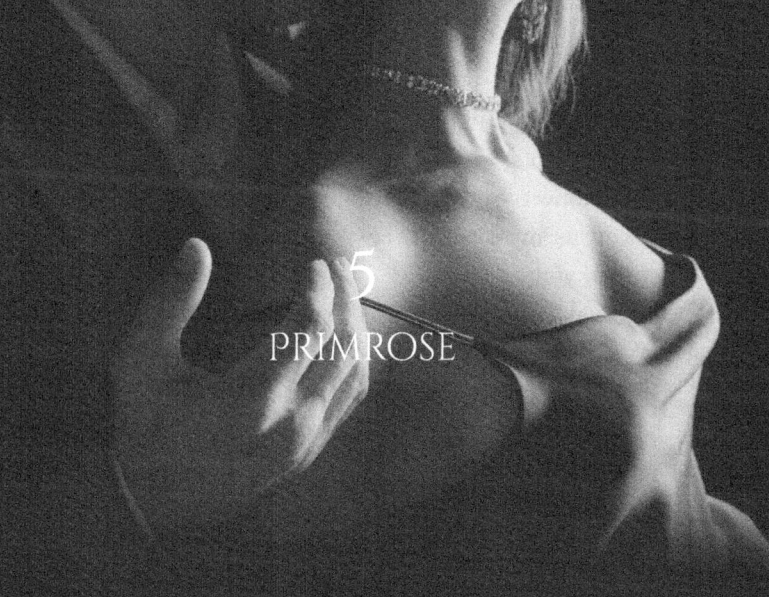

5
PRIMROSE

"I didn't even know fabric stores existed," Amiyah says as she runs her finger across tulle.

Brixley frowns at Amiyah, slight judgment on her face. "You've never been to a fabric store?"

Amiyah shakes her head. "No, I've never had to make anything myself. Of course, I've seen rolls of fabric from doing plays and things at school, but I thought, well..." She laughs a little at herself. "I've never thought about where it came from."

I pick white tulle and satin, long rolls of lace, stacking them in my cart. Grabbing five rows of string to help hide the seams. Next, I grab black lace to make the girls' bridesmaid dresses. I'm not particularly happy about my situation but this gives me a huge distraction from everything going on in my life. And maybe Vance is right, the devil I know is better than the one I don't.

"Prim, are you okay?" Brixley asks, rubbing my shoulder.

I shrug. "There isn't anything I can do about the situation besides run away. And where would I go where he won't be able to find me?" I know it sounds as if I've given up. Maybe I have.

"I'm honestly at a loss for words. On one hand, do I want you as my sister-in-law? Of course, but not at the expense of your freedom."

"Agreed," Amiyah says. "If you want to disappear, I can make it happen, love."

"I don't want to. Vance and I have been circling around each other for a year now, maybe this is how it was always meant to be?"

"Maybe," they both whisper quietly.

The truth is, I don't know what I want. I'm so heartbroken and confused, and on top of that I'm still grieving my mother. So, for now, I plan to go with the flow. I can always file for divorce later down the road.

"You know what? Let's go drink," Amiyah says as we walk out with way too much fabric but, who cares?

"First off, it's eleven in the morning," Brixley says.

"Actually, that sounds great." I smile.

OF COURSE, IT'S A STRIP CLUB—SORRY, EXOTIC DANCE CLUB. I'M not sure how many drinks I've had but I feel fuzzy, and my cheeks hurt from smiling as well. Amiyah and Brixley are laughing with me as Beckett glares from the corner of our booth. We couldn't escape him.

"Oh my god, I love this song," Brix says, standing up and dancing.

Brixley and I are totally lightweights compared to Amiyah, who is drinking straight from some expensive bottle of gin. Brixley pulls me up as I giggle, dancing with her. "Strip, strip," Amiyah chants, and Beckett glares at her.

"Don't even think about it, Rabbit. You either, Primrose."

I flip my hair over my shoulder, feeling wild and brave. "Come on, Brix. He's not the boss of us, let's get on the stage."

Amiyah cheers as I take a step onto the platform. I turn to face her, only for my world to be tipped upside down over a strong broad shoulder. "You've had enough." The deep voice sends shivers up my body as I stare at his dark laced boots. "Thanks for letting me know, Beck," Vance says as I peek up to glare at Beckett.

Beckett smirks, his eyes shining as he says, "No problem."

"I should put you in the trunk," Vance mumbles as he walks me to the car.

"I will fight you."

He chuckles. "Feeling feisty, baby girl? You know that makes me hard. So, by all means, fight me," he rasps.

I swallow, my stomach pooling with heat, slipping into my core and washing over my thighs at his words. My body lands in the super sleek blacked-out car. Vance climbs in and I grab his wrist. "Wait, my fabrics."

"I've already gotten it," he says, throwing the car into drive and pulling out of the parking lot.

I cover my eyes with my arms to block out the afternoon sun. "Where are we going?"

"I'm taking you home and throwing you in the shower so you can sober up. And then, we are going to have dinner with my parents."

The last thing I should be worried about is what his parents think of me, and yet, I do. A small part of me wants them to like me. Wants to be welcomed into a new family. "Okay. It's still early so I should be able to take a nap as well, right?"

He looks over to me, unamused and irritated. "Yeah, you should do that."

I REMEMBER THE SMELL OF METALLIC BLOOD AS IT SEEPED through the air. Devlin made us watch as he played Edward Scissorhands with Brixley's body. I remember not being able to move but screaming for help. The drug he gave Amiyah and me paralyzed us until finally, we passed out.

When I wake up, I hear voices, but my eyes quickly jerk to the cross I had last seen Brixley on, only to find it empty. Vance sits beneath it, a limp, unrecognizable body in his hands as he works the emotions back down his throat. Beckett's voice pulls me away from Vance to watch as Devlin holds a gun to Beckett's head. I stare wide-eyed, wanting to do something but having no clue what, until I hear her.

My best friend proclaiming she is going to kill Devlin.

I don't think, I move, knocking Brixley away from the gunshot as hot, unbearable pain explodes on my face. I scream, clutching my cheek, as red blood spills between my fingers.

My body shoots up, eyes blurry as I clutch my cheek, a hot, warm body wrapped around mine as I hyperventilate. "He's dead and you're fine," Vance says softly next to my ear.

"It always feels so real, like I'm living that hell all over again," I confess as Vance gently pulls my hand from my cheek.

"I know that what you went through would break most grown men but—"

"He made us watch," I cut him off. Confused as to why I'm confessing this to him. "He made us watch as he cut up Brixley's face. I swear her screams will never leave my memory for as long as I live. The smell of blood that lingered in the air, the wild look in his eyes as he gutted her. And I couldn't do anything but watch. Paralyzed by the drugs in my system. I never want to feel that helpless again, Vance."

Vance kisses the top of my head. "And you won't. After this wedding is over with, I'll train you."

I peek up at him, biting back a smile. "You will?"

He nods. "The world you're about to enter is brutal, why would I leave you defenseless?" He stands, stretching his arms above his head. "Now, we need to get ready."

Samson jumps on the bed, cuddling up in my lap as I pet his midnight fur. "Okay," I whisper.

Vance leaves and I pull a light pink silk dress from my closet, laying it on the bed. Walking over to my vanity, I turn my curling iron on. I slip the dress on, not bothering to look in the mirror. I avoid looking myself in the face until I have to do my makeup. Sitting down, I divide my hair, adding heat protectant before twirling it around the curler. Once I've finished, I run my fingers through the curls to give them some volume. And then finally, I look at the mirror and the sight alone makes me want to throw my fist through it. My hand shakes as I hold my beauty blender with my perfectly matching shade of foundation on it. Strong fingers wrap around my wrist, squeezing until I drop the sponge. Vance peers behind me in the mirror, reaching over my shoulder, he grabs my makeup bag. Walking to the balcony, I watch in shock as he throws the whole bag over the edge.

"Vance." I stand. "Why did you do that?"

He turns to look at me. "I'm tired of seeing you cake that shit on. Besides, you don't need it. Fuck what people think about your scar." He walks over to the bed, grabbing my heels and stalking toward me. He gently pushes me down onto the vanity seat and gets on his knees to place my heels on my feet. "You have killer legs, Primrose. I often picture them wrapped around my head." My cheeks heat, allowing him to distract me from the fact that he just tossed hundreds of dollars' worth of makeup over the balcony. "What do you say?" He looks up, smirking as his fingers walk a path up the inside of my thigh. "When we get back, you let me live out my fantasy?"

I bat his hands away, standing. "We're going to be late."

It's oddly freeing knowing that even though my makeup is gone, he still has fantasies about me. I honestly believe he was marrying me out of pity, but maybe, just maybe, he still finds me attractive.

AURORA DE LUCA IS BEAUTIFUL AND TIMELESS, AND I SEE THE TINY hints of Brixley in her, even though I'll never confess that to my best friend. "Oh, wow," Aurora gushes, holding my hand as she takes me in. She smiles over my shoulder at Vance, "She's beautiful."

I blush at the compliment, but also, in the back of my mind, there is a little voice that says she's lying. "Thank you."

"No thanks needed. Vance, your father is in the study, be so kind as to disappear as I get to know my new daughter and talk weddings."

"Mother," Vance says.

"Do not mother me, son. Shoo." I giggle as she pretends to swat him away. Aurora walks me through the foyer and into a sitting room where two glasses of wine await us. "Now," she says, taking a seat opposite of me. "Tell me about your family, your major. All the things."

I clear my throat. "My father is a contractor and my mother..." I trail off, blinking fast so the tears will evaporate. "She recently died. Cancer."

Aurora places a hand to her chest, sitting her wine glass down as she finds my free hand. "Oh, sweetheart, I am so very sorry for your loss."

"Thank you." I smile politely. "As for my major." I try to change the topic quickly. As to not cry. "I'm getting a fashion degree." I shrug. "I know it seems silly, but I truly love making clothes."

"A fashion designer. Wow, that's actually amazing. I've been looking for a new designer, you must show me your portfolio someday."

My chest warms and a real smile breaks across my stiff lips. "I'd love that."

"So, wedding plans are not out of your element?" she asks.

"Not at all. I was thinking lavender and black. Something to showcase me as well as Vance. I was thinking black roses with lavender sparling tips." I shrug. "I don't know."

"Oh, but I love this. We could do gothic meets feminism." She claps once. "Yes, and your dress?"

"I'm designing it. I got the fabrics today. Do you... do you want to see?"

Aurora grins. "Of course."

"Hold on, I need to go get them from the trunk of the car." I rise, making my way to the hall, when a dark figure stops me.

"Where are you going, Miss Thatcher?" Adriano asks.

"To get my fabrics out of the trunk."

He holds up a hand. "No need, I'll go get it."

Glaring, I pull out my phone.

Me: I don't appreciate your henchman following me around.

Vance: Get used to it.

Me: Whatever.

Vance: That sass.

I roll my eyes, waiting on Adriano to bring my fabrics in, and follow behind him until he sets them down. "Thanks. I don't think you need to keep watching me in my own future in-laws' house."

Adriano shrugs. "Boss says I do."

Aurora laughs. "Might as well save your energy on this battle."

Adriano leaves and I look over to Aurora. "It's just annoying."

She takes a sip of her wine. "Trust me, I know. Now, tell me about this dress."

And so, I do. Drawing a quick sketch of what I am envisioning until we are called to dinner.

Maybe my new family won't be so bad, after all.

6
VANCE

I SMIRK at the text on my screen. No way in hell my *henchman* won't be following her every move when I can't physically do it myself. After the whole Devlin shit show, there will not be a point in this lifetime where I do not have eyes on Primrose.

I wish I could bring that motherfucker back to life just so I could have my turn to kill him. It's not only because he terrorized my angel, but holding my unrecognizable baby sister in my arms, not sure if she was alive or dead, made something inside me snap. All the things I've patched up in my life slowly unraveled as I looked down to my bloody spitfire. I had just gotten her back after so long, and Devlin thought he could just take her from me again? Fuck that. If Brixley hadn't killed him, I would have. Only, it would have been a slow, painful death. I'd take a chapter out of the medieval book of torture I love to read. But she did, killed that fucker, because Brixley Archer is a badass.

My father clears his throat as I sit in his office. Lost in thought of a vengeance I'll never get to fulfill. Money cannot in fact buy everything. I look up, meeting the dark eyes of an older version of my face. I raise an eyebrow. "Would you like to enlighten me on what was going through that mind of yours when you decided to let a debt slip? All for some girl?"

My jaw tightens. "I don't have to explain myself to you. We both know that. Marriage is the one thing you've allowed me complete freedom in."

"True." He pushes a cigar in his mouth, looking like an old gangster in a movie. "But when it comes to money, that's my business. You don't rule this kingdom yet."

I shrug. "It's already done."

"It can be undone," he deadpans.

I grind my teeth. "No, because I will not allow it to be. She's mine now."

My father narrows his eyes. "I expect an heir within the first year."

I laugh, shaking my head. "Yeah, sure." I pluck a cigarette out, pushing it between my lips and lighting it. "Only, that's also my decision. The only requirement I am to achieve is that I'm married before taking the crown from you. An heir was never in your twisted rules."

My father sighs. "As true as that may be, I would like to be a grandfather before I keel over, or someone puts a bullet between my eyes."

"Not my problem, you should have had more children."

He laughs, the sound raspy and light. "You were plenty. Now," he rises, "let's go eat this dinner and you allow me to meet my new daughter."

I stand, putting my cigarette in the ashtray. "Let's."

What is she thinking? It's something I've wondered since I first laid eyes on her. I watch as she sips hot chocolate on the back porch overlooking the forest. The sun is just peeking over the tops of the dark trees. Samson lays in her lap, tail moving slowly back and forth. Primrose tilts her head at the cat. I watch as her mouth moves, talking to him. *Lucky bastard.* The only time she speaks to me is to start a fight. Not that I blame her. I didn't expect her to be happy with this arrangement, but taking in our history, I never dreamed she'd take this long to actually look me in the eyes. I long to be in the public eye, because in public, like last night with my parents, she speaks to me, looks at me with wonder in her eyes like she did once upon a time.

I open the door, walking onto the porch. Primrose stiffens, looking over her shoulder. As soon as she sees me, she rises. Samson meows in protest as he falls on his tiny paws in front of her. "Sit," I command, and like the obedient angel she is, she does, huffing.

I take the seat across from her, bending my head to light the smoke in my mouth. "Those things kill, you know," she informs me.

I grin around my cigarette. "I'm already dead."

She narrows her eyes. "May I leave now?"

"Not quite. We need to talk."

She sighs, dropping her chin on her hand as she looks past me at the sunset. "What about?"

"Our situation wasn't ideal, I get that, but I can't keep watching you walk around like you're a prisoner."

"That's what I am, though," she says lowly. "I traded one cage for another, just like I always knew I would. I thought if I got into The Misfits, I could become powerful and take my own life into my hands. But as fate would have it, you are a Misfit and the De Luca mafia. There is no escaping that."

I release a puff of smoke, not liking how she's looking at the situation. "You're not a fucking prisoner, you're going to be my wife, one of the most powerful women in this country."

"What's the point in having this power if you have no freedom to wield it?" she asks, finally looking at me, and the nothingness in her stare guts me.

"If you're looking for pity, for me to release you, it's not happening."

"I know."

"You act as if the sexual tension between us is null, as if we haven't been skating around each other for months."

"Until I fucked another, correct? Then I was on my own to face your wrath," she snaps.

I throw my smoke to the ground, trapping it beneath my boot. "That's right, Angel. You should have never allowed another to touch what is mine." I growl. "And you sure as fuck should have not reminded me of that fact. But here is the thing, I don't care how many cocks you've sucked, how many have been all up inside your tight pussy, because at the end of the day, you're still mine."

Her cheeks flush at my words and she looks away.

"What's the matter?" I taunt. "You can fuck other guys, see their weak example of what a man is, but the word cock makes you blush?" I chuckle, standing. I move until I'm in front of her, hands braced on each side of her body as I lean in. "When I'm finally inside you, I'm going to rip what's left of your innocence to shreds."

She swallows. "Are we through?" she asks, still refusing me those glaciers.

I smile. "With this conversation? Sure. With us? Not by a long shot."

"I don't think that punching bag has done anything to you," Beckett comments as we work out in my home gym.

"Shut up," I snarl, punching the bag harder. Thinking of Primrose with other men has me murderous as fuck.

"Fine. I do want to run something by you. There is land besides yours and I'm thinking of buying it and building a house."

I stop the bag in my grasp, resting my head against the cool leather as I catch my breath. "Just say you're obsessed with me."

Beckett chuckles. "Your sister wants to be closer to you. If it were up to me, we'd live in the city."

"Why don't you grow a pair and tell her that?"

"Because, this is Brixley's world, I'm just living in it, happily."

I look over to him, my eyes narrowed. Will I ever be so helplessly in love that I give up all my freedom? It seems as if Beckett compromises so much, but I'm not in their relationship. I shake my head, grabbing a towel and running it over my sweaty face. I look down to my Apple Watch, spotting the time and cursing. "I've got to go."

I walk out of my gym, heading up the stairs quickly, stopping at Primrose's door. I bang on it loudly. She swings the door open, hair a mess and dress crumpled. "Did you take a nap?" I ask.

She crosses her small arms over her chest, my eyes

dropping and holding on the swell that peeks from the top of her tank top. "Yes, is that a problem?"

I bite my lip to keep it from tipping into a smile. "Nah, Angel. But get ready."

Her brow furrows, her lip doing that cute pouting thing it does when she's confused. "Why?"

"We're going out."

I walk away, leaving her quietly fuming in her doorway.

I have to find a way to get over her betrayal, since we are going to spend the rest of our lives together.

And it's time she accepts that.

7
VANCE

Age nine

I squeeze my eyes together, hiding my head under the blanket and trying to even my breaths. I know it won't work, though. She doesn't care what stage I'm in, sleeping, awake, or even conscious. I wish Mom and Dad would make her get a hotel, but they never do, it's not the famiglia way.

Aunt Lucia and I have a secret. She says it's not bad, but no one would understand our love. The thing is, I don't understand our love. She makes me do things... things I don't want to do. She touches me. I know it's inappropriate, I'm old enough to realize it, but what kind of man would I be if I told anyone about it? Everyone would look at me as a weak child. Someone who can easily be taken advantage of. So, I stay quiet.

It started a year ago. Aunt Lucia stumbled into my room drunk, saying it would be a one-time thing. I was confused and when she reached her hands into my pants, gripping me, I became ashamed. She told me if I told, that Father and Mother would send me away and I wouldn't get to see my little sister anymore. Another reason I stayed quiet.

It was never a one-time thing; it happens every time she's

here. It went from her touching me to her forcing me to touch her. I hate it, it grosses me the fuck out.

My door creaks and I curse under my breath. "Vance." I used to find her voice sweet but now I feel sick every time I hear it. "It's time to play."

I will kill her someday.

PRESENT

My jaw tightens as I stare Aunt Lucia down in the restaurant. *What the fuck is she doing here?*

She smiles and I grimace, my stomach twisting in knots. Old memories fly back into my mind and I try my hardest to fight them off. "Vance... are you okay?"

Primrose's voice is like a beacon of light in my dark mind, and I lower my eyes to her concerned face. "Yeah, why?"

She adjusts her hair over her scarred cheek. "It's just... you broke the glass in your hand. You're bleeding."

I look down and see the shattered glass, tiny shards poking from my hand as specks of blood flows from different spots. *So, I have.* I meet her eyes, but quickly break the contact. "Just lost in my own thoughts."

The waiter rushes over, cleaning my mess and setting a first aid kit down. Primrose rises, coming to my side of the table, and kneels before me, her hair hiding her face as she inspects my hand. The odd thing about Primrose, she's the only person who can touch me and it does not burn. It's not comfortable, per say, I still want to push her the fuck away, but it's bearable. My brain is fucked. I can touch people, but if someone touches me, it's like liquid fire. The therapist I used to have said it's because I'm in control that way. Either way, it makes for a difficult sexual encounter.

Primrose opens the first aid kit. "They're not deep at least," she muses before she begins to clean the small cuts. I shake my head when she gets the Band-Aids out. There is no fucking way I'm walking around with Band-Aids on my hands. I cup her face, pulling her to look at me. My hand moves over the scar, loving the roughness on such a delicate creature. "Thank you, Angel."

She smiles, pulling away from me. "It's no problem."

I watch as she takes her seat again, sipping her water as she looks at the white tablecloth in front of her. I open my mouth to speak, when a hand lands on my shoulder. The smell of her expensive perfume makes my stomach coil and my hands shake slightly. "Been a while, has it not?" If a voice could trigger the need to throw up, it would be hers.

I shrug her hand off my shoulder, keeping my eyes on my only restraint. Primrose looks to me and then to Lucia, frowning. "What do you want, Lucia?"

She tuts, I can imagine her pouting, but I refuse to look at her face. "Just to see how my favorite nephew is doing." I grind my teeth, willing the tremble in my hands to stop. "And who do we have here?" she asks.

"Future wife," Primrose surprises me by saying, holding her left hand up to shake hers. "Primrose, and you are?" She smiles sweetly. But something in her eyes seems a little dark. As if she picked up on how uncomfortable I am.

"Lucia, Vance's aunt. I heard he was engaged, but I was expecting something... well, more."

"Watch how you speak to my future wife," I snap, turning to stare Lucia down.

She smiles at that. "It wasn't an insult."

"Well, as much as I love family reunions." I wave the

waiter over for the check. "We are leaving, unfortunately. So kindly, fuck off."

Lucia grins. "I'll be seeing you around, Vance."

Not if I kill you first.

"Vance," Primrose says as we sit on the back porch, eating hamburgers. Our night out was officially ruined as soon as I saw *her*. And fuck, I wish she didn't have that much power over me.

"Sup, baby girl?"

"Was my father really trying to sell me off? It's not that I didn't know this would happen, it's just, he promised I could finish school first."

I love the delicacy of her voice; I wish she'd talk to me all day, every day, even if it's only to ask me questions, which she does do often if we are in public. "Yeah, to some very nasty old men. He looks at you as if you're ruined now."

"And you," I look over to her sparkling eyes, "do you look at me as if I'm ruined?"

I shake my head, making sure our eyes bleed into one another's, when I whisper, "I could never."

"Then why? Why did you choose to take me?"

I toss my half-eaten food into the bag, opting for a cigarette. "The mafia has rules, and my family has rules. When I graduate next year, I'll be taking over the kingdom. In order to do that, I have to be married first. So, I saw an opportunity and I took it."

"Even though I'm not pure?"

"You could fuck a hundred guys and I'd still take you, Primrose."

"But why?"

"I don't fucking know," I mumble around my cigarette.

"Do you think this marriage will ever have room for love?"

I tilt my head at the moon. "I'm not sure I'm capable of love. Obsession? Sure. But love... I'll never allow myself to be that vulnerable."

"Why—"

I cut her off, it's my turn to ask some questions. "No, why did you give away your virginity to some stranger?"

She looks to her lap, sighing deeply. "I wanted to push you away."

"Why?"

"Because I knew that it wouldn't matter if we started something, because we could never be. I've known my whole life I wouldn't marry for love."

"Are you done fighting me, Primrose?"

She nods.

"Come here."

8
PRIMROSE

As I ate quietly, I thought of the way Vance seemed to shrink into himself as his aunt approached. I've never seen him that way and it scared me.

Almost as much as right now.

Sitting next to him on the outdoor love seat, my breaths become choppy as he leans closer. "I just want to forget for a little while, can you help me do that, Angel?" The desperation in his voice has me nodding. There is pain in his eyes as they slowly close, not allowing me into the windows of his soul.

My eyes flutter at the first brush of his full, warm lips. His five-o'clock shadow scratches against me. I gasp, my mouth falling open slightly as my toes curl. Secret? This is my first kiss. I never dreamed it could be... like this. Trying to explain this warm, gooey feeling... it's impossible. His tongue takes over my mouth, stroking softly. My hands land on his chest and suddenly, his fingers are wrapping around my wrists, slowly pinning them to my thighs. Vance's forehead rests on mine, our breaths mixing. "You can't touch me."

My bottom lip pokes out just a bit. "Why?"

"I don't like to be touched."

My eyebrows scrunch together in confusion. I've seen Brixley touch him multiple times. "Why?"

He sighs. "For once, don't be so curious and just do as I say."

"I can't help it."

His hands curl into mine, pulling them up above my head as he pushes me gently to the cushions. With my hands restrained above my head, he lays on top of me. "I know, baby girl."

His lips crash back to mine, harsher, hungrier. Desperate. This is what I expected kissing Vance would be like. So wild and untamed it would make your heart explode. Something unfamiliar begins to build, throbbing like a pulse between my legs. Vance breaks from my mouth, his lips trailing down my neck and laying suckling kisses to the tender flesh. One of his hands cups both wrists while the other holds on to my waist, before slowly making a trail down my hip and slipping under my dress at my thighs.

Panic hits me. My eyes shoot open, and I pause. "Wait."

Vance tilts his head. "Why?"

"Because I…" I need a lie—I'm a terrible liar and he knows it. "I haven't shaved." I want to grin in triumph at how smoothly the lie fell off my tongue.

Vance grins. "Hair doesn't bother me, Angel."

His hand travels higher and I try to wiggle from his grip.

"I'm not ready," I blurt.

Vance stops, murderous eyes drilling into me. "I want to get something straight. You were ready for him, but not me? The man you will be spreading these milky thighs for, for the rest of your life. The only man. Do I understand you correctly?"

His mouth is so sinfully dirty, I want to hate it, but I can't. I swallow, nodding. "Yes."

He scoffs, lifting off of me. "Whatever you say, Angel. We need to go to sleep anyways."

"Why?"

"We're going golfing in the morning."

"But I don't like to golf," I yell to his back.

"Too fucking bad."

"I think space will do us good. We don't have to do everything together, you know."

He laughs, stopping and turning to brace his hands on the doorframe. "Yeah, the fuck we do." And then he's gone.

And I'm left with an ache I don't think my tiny fingers can cure.

GOLFING IS ONE OF THE LEAST EXCITING THINGS I'VE EVER endured in my life. And worse, Vance's clothes. He looks so out of sorts with them on. I know he doesn't only wear all black with a leather jacket twenty-four seven, I've seen him in a suit and tie, but this is strange. Khaki trousers, a brown belt, and a white polo with a white dad hat. I watch as he lines the driver—I think that's what he's been going on about all morning—up and the whacks the tiny white-and-black golf ball. Apparently, they come in all colors. Who knew? Not me. I don't know a single thing about this sport. He told me I was his caddie, but I've yet to lift a single finger. We both watch the ball travel far until we can no longer see it. Vance walks back to the golf cart, setting his club in the bag and climbing into the driver's seat. "Primrose."

I turn and am met with soft lush lips against my own. I gasp, pulling back. "What was that for?" I ask, my heart doing a tiny flip.

"Just taking it slow so you'll be *ready* for me."

I ponder that as we drive to wherever the ball landed. I have no clue but Vance drives with purpose. Once he stops, I turn in the seat to face him. "If you're going to be crossing my boundaries, I'll cross yours."

"I enjoy a good challenge, baby. What do you have for me?"

My hand reaches his and I feel him flinch. "I'm going to touch you."

He pulls his hand away from me, the sudden movement knocking his sunglasses down to his nose. "I'll give you anything and everything, but that."

I bite my lip. "Why don't you like people to touch you? I've seen people touch you and you act fine."

"On the outside. But I'm going to be really fucking blunt with you, every touch feels like a burn."

My chest aches and I ask what I've been wondering since last night. "Did someone hurt you?"

He laughs. "As if they could. I just don't like being touched."

"Vance, if I can't touch you, how will we ever... you know?"

He grins. "Fuck?" I bristle at his crass language. "I have *techniques* for that."

And then he's off, finding his stupid ball on a course that's going to take all day. I may not have loved the idea of marrying Vance, but I've accepted it. I plan to give him hell, but ultimately, I know this is my life now. But I'm a hopeless romantic, and if this is for life, I want it to be real.

"You're a little sunburned," Vance comments as we sit down at the country club restaurant to eat.

I shrug. "It doesn't matter, I can't get a tan to save my life."

I watch as Vance stretches his arms on the table, and I take the opportunity to look at his hands. Not that I haven't seen them before, but it was almost as if I was too scared to get to know any part of him. His right hand has a skull tattoo with a black bandana covering its mouth. His left hand has a black-and-gray rose with a single bullet laid under it. Something in Italian scrawled across the side. But on both sets of his fingers, they're blank. For a man who is covered in tattoos, you would think when he got the tops of his hands done, he would have done his knuckles. "Why are your fingers blank?" I blurt out. I'm a very curious person. Always asking why, never stopping to think if it might be inappropriate.

Vance pauses, the glass of water close to his lips, arching an eyebrow. "Saving it for something special."

I purse my lips. "What will it be?" I ask.

"I'll let you know when I figure that out." He watches me as he takes a long drink of his water. I watch his Adam's apple bob under the thick column of his inked skin. The wolf on his neck is impossible to miss with its snarling nose and sharp teeth. It's one of my favorite tattoos of his. Maybe because it's the only one I've truly seen. Anytime he's shirtless, I blush and look away. "Thinking about getting another tattoo?" he asks, making my eyes jerk away from his hypnotizing neck.

I wait patiently in my room as Vance tattoos Brixley downstairs. It wasn't ever mentioned that a tattoo was required. Not a single word was spoken of it. It's not as if I'm scared, I just never looked at myself as someone getting a tattoo. Vance opens the door, glaring at me as he shuts it behind me. It's been like this since I had Cooper over. He's been cold but never too far behind. Like he can't help himself, making sure I'm okay. I look away as he sits down, getting his tattoo gun ready. "Where do you want it?" His gruff voice skates across my skin.

I blush, but the spot I've chosen will be the easiest place to hide it. "Underside of my breasts."

Vance coughs, clearing his throat. "You'll have to take your bra off for that and raise your dress."

I swallow. Slipping my hands behind my back, I undo my bra. Letting the straps fall down my arms as I yank it off under my dress, allowing it to fall to the ground. Vance's phone begins playing "Man in the Box" by Alice in Chains. I look up to see his hungry eyes watching me. I straighten my shoulders, pretending like I'm not blushing. I walk slowly to the bed, laying back. Slowly, I lift my dress up, exposing my light pink cotton underwear. I really believed I could be brave, look him in the eyes as I exposed myself, but I can't, so I look away as I hold the dress up high until the underside of my breasts are exposed. Vance gently moves my hands, his own brushing lightly against my ribs until it traces up the swell of my breasts. My eyes close as his breath skates over my skin. His hand lightly keeping my breasts up so he can tattoo me. "Fuck." His low gruff voice comes right before the machine starts.

I shake my head slightly. "I'm not sure. I wish I could see them on me before I decide to commit to them for life."

"I can draw them on you." He grins, eyes tracing down my face and landing on where my Misfits tattoo lays under my clothes.

I blush, again. My body is so expressive for him, and I hate it. "So, you and Beckett are both into art? Can draw?"

Vance shakes his head. "Some may say so. Beckett is into sketching, I'm into tattoos."

I furrow my brow. "Is it not the same thing?" I ask, confused, because in my mind it is.

Vance laughs. "Not at all. He could never do what I do."

I ponder over that. I'm sure a live canvas is much harder. It moves, it has curves and scars. Not really an option for flat surfaces. "Is tattooing something you will pursue in the future?"

He shrugs. "I'm a businessman. I'll probably open a shop or two up, but ultimately, I'll be overlooking the strip clubs and illegal gambling rings. Lots of underground businesses. Drugs and gun trades, those sorts of things."

I look at him in horror. "I thought those were only rumors."

He raises an eyebrow. "What kind of life have you lived?"

"A sheltered one, obviously." I fidget with the hem of my dress uncomfortably.

"Don't panic, Angel. I'll keep you safe."

He's told me that before and last time, I was shot in the face. He must read my doubt because his eyes darken, and he leans over the table. "That was a one-off."

I nod, touching the scar. "Do you kill people?"

He sits back in his chair, and I'm thankful for the empty dining room. "I have."

"And why do they call you the De Luca Devil?" I swallow, not sure if I really want to know. By nature, I know I have to.

He rubs his bottom lip, watching me. "Because I ruin

people's lives. And when I do kill, it looks like an animal attack." I shiver. "But you have nothing to be afraid of. I'll never hurt you."

Better the devil you know, they say. Problem is, I'm not sure I truly know mine.

9
PRIMROSE

I ENJOY MY CAT. I enjoy music and sewing. Running first thing in the morning with Brixley, however, is not my favorite thing. But we've been doing it since we became roommates. It's our thing, unfortunately. Brixley stops at the edge of a trail on the mountain, catching her breath as she looks over the foggy view of the trees. And then, she screams. She screams so long and loud I grow worried. Frozen in shock.

She turns to me. "I liked my original nose," she says on a shaky exhale.

My face is bad, but it has no comparisons to Brixley's after Devlin was done with her. She had to go through so many facial reconstruction surgeries, we lost count. "I think both noses are great."

She rolls her eyes. "Get mad, Prim. Scream at the top of your lungs, let all the pain out." I step next to her and let a little scream out. Brix shakes her head. "No, let that shit out, Prim. He shot your face, your mom died, my brother is forcing you into a marriage. Let. It. Out."

I turn to the trees and close my eyes as I take a deep

breath. And then I scream. I let all the sadness and anger out. I feel the strings in my heart tear and then snap along with my knees. I buckle to the rocky ground as arms come around me. "There you go, Prim," Brixley says soothingly.

I didn't expect to feel anything, maybe more pain, but instead I feel a little lighter. "Thanks, Brix."

I SIT IN THE CAR I TECHNICALLY STOLE FROM VANCE. I STARE AT the church where it all happened. The history of this place is dark. Its energy only allows more darkness to swallow anyone who enters. This was once Brixley's favorite place, but even she doesn't come here anymore. The outside of the old church looks worn and so out of date I'm not sure how it's standing, but the inside has been updated a little. This is The Misfits' place. Where they conduct meetings and trials to see who will get in. But for me, a place I found such freedom in now holds my restraints. I wish it would disappear.

The passenger door opens and Vance slides in, hitting me with an unamused glare. "Couldn't find you. You know I don't like not having eyes on you at all times." I shrug, not commenting. "What are you doing here, Angel?"

"Wishing this place would disappear," I say quietly.

"You want it gone?" I nod. "Then it's gone." Vance pulls out his phone, calling Adriano, my watchdog, no doubt. "Yeah, bring some gasoline and torches." He pauses. "The fuck does it seem like we're about to do? Also, I'd like to discuss why you're not with my future wife. You had one job. Fucking idiot," he mumbles as he ends the call, throwing the car door open.

"Where are you going?"

He braces his hands on the top of the car, bending down to look at me. "To get Beckett's beloved cross out of there. I'm not listening to him bitch." He taps the roof of the car. "Be right back." And then he's gone.

VANCE HANDS ME A SINGLE MATCH. "DO THE HONORS, ANGEL. Light this bitch up."

I scrape the match against the scratch patch and watch the flame before flicking it at the open door. I watch the flame catch fire and a small smile breaks across my face. Adriano takes a torch, lighting it around the outside of the church, and before long the entire church building is all up in bright warm flames. Vance steps up to me and I slip my hand in his, and he stiffens but he doesn't break away from me.

"Does this make you happy?" he asks.

"It's a start," I whisper.

"Good."

We watch as the church crumbles to the ground, our hands interlocked the entire time. Until Vance shatters my peace. "Our wedding is next week."

I look up to him, glaring. "How long have you had a date?"

"Since before I showed up at your house."

I look away, having the strong urge to hit him. "Good thing my dress is almost ready and your mom handled all the arrangements. A heads-up would have been nice, though."

"You were just starting to like me again," he says simply.

"Way to ruin that." I go to jerk my hand from his, but he clutches onto me tighter.

"Just... can we not fight right now? It's such a beautiful sight," he says.

"Yeah," I whisper.

It truly is.

I STARE DOWN AT MY PHONE AS AMIYAH LAYS ON A LOUNGE CHAIR in big sunglasses and a floppy hat. She and Madden went to their family vacation home for the summer. I'm hoping those two don't kill each other. They glare at one another and barely talk unless Madden wants to boss her around. And if you know Amiyah, you know that doesn't go over well.

"Wait, you just found out yesterday your wedding is next week?"

"Yep," I grind out.

"That bastard. I've had my invitation for a month." she says, sipping on a glass of lemon water. "Good news, I'll be in early and you, Brixley, and I will be going out on a little bachelorette party." She smiles brightly, her golden skin shimmering under the bright sun. She looks happy at least.

"What do you have in mind?" I ask, a little worried.

She pulls her sunglasses down to the tip of her nose. "It won't be none of that old lady shit you're into. No bird watching or puzzles. No, you're going to live a little, but that part is a surprise."

We chat a little longer until finally hanging up. I go back

to work on my dress. I haven't slept since Vance told me last night. This is the one thing I have control of, and I want it to be perfect. It has to be. *I wish Momma could see this.* My nose stings and I shake the thought away. I look over to her silk dress. I don't want to destroy it. I just can't, but I can take silk from the underskirt and the brooch pinned to it. I plan to use the silk on my bouquet and as a sash to my dress. The brooch I haven't quite figured out yet.

I startle when hot lips land on my neck, a strong hand combing through my hair. My eyes close as my head falls to the side, allowing him better access. His free hand trails over my neck, down the valley of my breasts, until he's slipping my dress up my thighs, bunching it at my waist.

"Vance," I try to protest but it comes out as a moan.

"You think your tight little pussy can take my cock after letting that fucker inside you?" He chuckles as my hands fall to my sides. "No," he whispers next to my ear as he wraps my wrist in sticky duct tape, pinning both my wrists together behind the back of the chair I'm in.

"What are you doing?" I ask, lost to the scent of him.

"Remember those techniques I mentioned? This is my favorite one. You can't touch me, Primrose."

Was this a form of torture? Is he teasing me? "But I want to."

"I know, baby girl," he says, sucking on my neck.

"Then you can't touch me," I say breathlessly. I want him to touch me, but I don't think this is fair.

His finger circles my entrance through my panties. "And what's going to stop me?"

"Morals?"

He chuckles, the richness of it caresses me as his five-o'clock shadow brushes over my neck. "I don't have those."

"You do for me," I state confidently.

"How about this, you let me get you ready to take my cock and we'll work on you touching me. How does that sound?" I nod, because no sound can come out. Not with his finger slowly pulling my panties to the side.

He rubs his thumb through my wet folds, and I gasp, jerking against the chair and my restraints. "Already so responsive, and I haven't even begun to touch you," he rasps. "Look at how your nipples shamelessly beg for attention through your dress." I don't look, not when he's circling my entrance with one finger while his thumb brushes lightly over my clit. He leans over, biting down on my erect nipple through my thin dress as he thrusts a finger inside me.

I gasp, my head falling back against the chair as something between a scream and a moan passes past my lips. He removes his finger from me, leaving behind a stinging ache. I'm not sure if it's pain or want. Or both.

I feel his hands on the collar of my dress. With a tug, he rips the material down the middle, my breasts freeing, exposed to his hungry gaze. I want to be ashamed, want to feel as if I wish I left my bra on, but all I feel is an incredible need between my thighs. "These are perfect," he whispers. Squeezing the right one roughly in his palm as pleasure and pain mix into something raw. "I'm going to fuck these." He squeezes both breasts in his palms, pinching my nipples between his fingers. "Someday soon."

I bite down on my lip as his left hand slides up to my neck and his other trails back to my aching core. My back arches as he slips two fingers inside of me, his hand tightly squeezing my neck and jerking my head toward his as his lips descend.

I have nothing to compare this experience to. The way my body flushes with wave after wave, how my hot, pulsing heat seems to want to trap his fingers inside me every time they leave me. I feel like I can't kiss him hard enough. This urge to bring him so close so there isn't a single inch of our body that doesn't touch as I grind myself against him. The compulsion, instant obsession, with a man I'm being forced to marry is so unexplainable. I want to scream his name, make sure my moans echo in his dreams. I want to be all he sees, but...

I moan as his thumb presses down on my clit and my body breaks. Like something leaves my soul as I shatter around his fingers, thrashing and shivering. Melting into his kiss as my body falls limp against the chair. My arms are sore from the fight I put up to touch him. I'm slick with sweat and my breaths are choppy. I feel so... I want more. More of him and what he can do to my body. "More," I whisper tightly.

"Already addicted to what I can give you, Primrose?" He chuckles, pulling my chair back and grabbing me by the waist, lifting me and my bound wrists easily. My heat hits rock-solid abs and I look down to take a peek. His chest is like a war zone of angels and demons. Harsh blacks and grays. I want to trace them, see what else decorates his body of art. The light catches slightly on the piercing on each of his nipples. Which is... so hot. I can't even with this man so far.

I fly backward, landing on my back as my hands get trapped behind me. I look up to see the cut of his broad shoulders, covered in intricate designs I can't make out from here. My eyes trace down his rose-covered arm, the sharp thorns so realistic I'm afraid if I touch it, it'll draw blood. His other arm is filled with attractive demonic women. One with horns and sharp teeth, another with her mouth stitched and her tongue peeking out. My favorite looks new. It's an angel with light hair, but she's pulling her mask off to reveal something dark inside. His abs are free of ink, displaying hard rolls of sculpted muscles, ending in a sharp V that defines his hip bones so spectacularly, you'd think he was carved from stone. On his lower abdomen, *Devil* is written in bold black script with a thin outline around the letters. Raven hair peeks from his sweats that hang low. I follow the hair up to his belly button. "Such a good girl, Primrose, but your body, your soul, is so fucking hungry you leak sex appeal from your pores. I can't wait to break open that appetite and let it feast on me. Now, if you're done eye fucking me, Angel, I'm going to reward you."

I look up, meeting deep, hauntingly beautiful eyes as they curve over my exposed body. "I'm done for now." Funny how I thought I could stop the attraction to this man.

Vance smirks. "I'm going to allow you to touch me."

"I have an idea. You have all these tattoos, I have a box of markers, why don't I color your tattoos? I think that's an easy way to start since a person holding a needle doesn't bother you."

He tilts his head at me, studying me. "I think we can start there."

He reaches out, latching onto my ankles, flipping me over in one move. I feel the knife cut through the tape. Once he's done, I roll back over, looking down at my wrists. "Did it hurt you?" he asks, grabbing my wrists and examining them.

'No," I say softly. Standing, I grab a pair of sleep pants and a tank. Plus, new panties because mine are wet and sticky between my thighs. I change in the bathroom quickly. Once I get done, I go to my desk and grab my box of

Sharpies. Climbing onto the bed. Vance lays stretched out on my mattress, staring at the ceiling. "Where do you want me to start?" I ask softly.

"My arm." He stretches his rose arm out for me.

Taking a deep breath, I pick out a soft lavender marker. I touch the tip of the marker to the rose at his wrist and Vance closes his eyes, his jaw hardening. "Did you know that stop signs were originally yellow?" I ask, watching his face. Samson jumps on the bed, curling into Vance's side. The traitor.

Vance cracks an eye open. "Come again?"

I nod. "I know, right? They believed the color yellow would grab drivers' attention, red wasn't an option since they didn't have a dye at the time that wouldn't fade, but they considered it. But in 1954 they finally had a fade-resistant paint and, lo and behold, red stop signs," I tell him this as I color the first rose.

"Tell me something else," he says, his body relaxing.

I purse my lips, scrunching my nose as I look through my markers and rack my brain for another fact. "Oh," I laugh. "How about this one, did you know it takes three hundred sixty-four licks to get to the center of a Tootsie Pop?"

"Did you test this, or..."

"Heck no. I don't have that kind of time on my hands." I trace the next rose in a bright blue.

"How do you know all of this?" he asks, his hand reaching out to tuck a piece of my hair behind my ear.

"Do you not have questions that need to be answered? My Google search history is wild."

He laughs as I sit the marker back, looking down at the two roses. "Are you done?" he asks.

"I don't want to overdo it." I look down at him. "But thank you for trusting me."

He looks down at his arm. "You want me to stay?"

I shake my head. "I think we've crossed enough boundaries for one night, don't you?"

He sighs, rising and stretching his arms. "Wouldn't mind crossing a few more, but I'll leave."

He turns to leave, when I stop him, "Hey, Vance?"

He looks over his shoulder. "Yeah, baby girl?"

"I'm still going to give you hell."

He grins, eyes shining bright. "I sure fucking hope so."

10
VANCE

For several weeks I've watch Primrose take fabrics and somehow create a magical vision of a dress. It started as a basic drawing. And then she was pinning fabrics to a mannequin. Her technique was complete madness, I had no clue what she was thinking. Not only that, but she also stopped halfway to create Amiyah's and Brixley's bridesmaids dresses. Only then did I have to make myself stop spying. My mother said something about bad luck. I don't believe in any type of luck, but I did want to be surprised when I saw her.

I button up my suit jacket in the mirror of the groom's suite. Madden and Beckett sit at the table, talking about their trip to the beach house this summer. I, on the other hand, will be on my honeymoon. There is no end date. Before classes start again, of course. But I want to spend as much time as I can with Primrose, save her from herself for a while.

Beckett looks up, meeting my eyes in the mirror. "Are you ready?"

Sighing, I say, "As I'll ever be."

We make our way out of the suite, and I smirk when I see Mr. Thatcher, his hand all bandaged up to hide his missing fingers. Madden frowns at him. "Looks like he was in an accident," he comments.

"Something like that," Beckett mumbles.

It feels like it takes forever to get to the ballroom the ceremony is being held in. The room screams gothic wedding with deep blacks and lavender purples. Black roses with lavender tips, black lace drapes along the chairs, white candles flickering along every available surface. Twinkling lights hang from the ceiling. There are small accents of lavender throughout, a true harsh contrast of the two people getting married here today. An old accordion begins playing a haunted version of "Here Comes the Bride". My lips twitch as I think of how much of me she put into a wedding she had no choice in. She's selfless to a fault. She could have made this wedding completely about her, and honestly, she should have, but she didn't.

The crowd turns as the big double doors open. Time moves slowly as I impatiently wait for my bride-to-be. I'm sure the flower girls were adorable, that my sister was a sight, but all I want at this moment is to see Primrose in white with my ring glistening on her finger. I pull on the collar of my black dress shirt. *Is it fucking hot in here? Why the fuck can I not breathe properly?* Time stills as I get the first glimpse of my angel. Tulle off-the-shoulder sleeves hanging loosely on her biceps. A sweetheart neckline that dips low into her cleavage, leaving nothing to the imagination of the lush flesh of her breasts. The bodice is all lace and silk underneath to hide the soft skin beneath. There is a vintage piece of cloth that makes a belt around her waist. From her mother's dress, I presume. The skirt is sheer tulle, hiding the parts that matter, but the slit up her right leg is sexy as fuck. And God, I'm getting a boner at the altar. I'd be worried if I were a godly man, but as rumor has it, I'm the devil.

I can't see her face due to the veil. I know she wanted to hide her face today, but that won't be fucking happening. I can see peeks of her light blonde hair hanging in loose curls. My fingers twitch to get my hands on her, to see her beautiful face, to run my fingers through the silky strands of her white hair and finally, fucking finally, lay my lips on hers, again.

Her father glares at me as he moves at a snail's pace down the aisle. He has a tight grip on her bicep with his uninjured hand. I zero in on his hand, and looking back to his eyes, I raise an eyebrow. Silently asking if he wants to lose his other fingers. He looks away, his grip loosening. Once she finally reaches me, I don't wait on the preacher to ask who gives the bride away, I pull her to me. Small body crashing into my chest as the scent of vanilla and roses fill my senses. She lets out a slight gasp. Small hands curling into my suit jacket as she looks up to me through a lace haze, and I wish I could see her face, but I hold it in. Her touch doesn't burn as much today, and for that I'm thankful, she's been drawling on my arm all week, telling me stupid facts no one should know.

I cradle her in my arms, not allowing any space between us even though it wouldn't be deemed acceptable, but fuck it. I look to the priest. "Proceed."

He swallows, visibly disturbed by my actions. He clears his throat and proceeds to drone on, but I tune him out, my full attention on the beautiful creature in front of me hidden behind the veil. She shakes slightly in my arms, and I lean closer, so only she can hear. "You're a sight to behold, Primrose Adonna." I watch her lips curl slightly and mine follow. I'm about to say something inappropriate, but the priest cuts me off.

"Do you, Vance Stefano De Luca, take this woman to be your wife, to live together in holy matrimony, to love her, to honor her, to comfort her, and to keep her in sickness and in health, forsaking all others, for as long as you both shall live?"

"I do," I say, placing the sparkling band onto her small, trembling finger.

"And do you, Primrose Adonna Thatcher, take this man to be your husband, to live together in holy matrimony, to love him, to honor him, to comfort him, and to keep him in sickness and in health, forsaking all others, for as long as you both shall live?"

I swear, everyone in attendance, including me, holds their breaths as we wait for her answer. She looks to me, her breathing coming in stronger as her chest moves rapidly. "I... I do."

The crowd sighs and a huge wolfish grin breaks across my face. "I now pronounce you man and wife. You may now kiss the bride."

I want to shred the veil, instead I lift it over her face, folding it over her hair. Her beautiful face greets me. Heavy lashes fan against her cheeks until she pops her glacier eyes open. Slight fear deep in the roots of them. I cup her face with both hands, bending my head until I finally feel her rose petal lips against mine, again. They're soft and full. She gasps slightly as I nibble on her bottom lip, coaxing her lips to open so I can slip my tongue in. She tastes so sweet I can't help but bite lightly on her tongue, marveling when I hear a slight moan fall between her delicate lips. Her hands curl into my suit, pulling me closer. I wish we were anywhere but here so I could skate my hands along this dress, slip my hand inside the slit and see if she wants me as bad as I want her.

The crowd breaks out into a cheer, and I finally pull back from her. "Here's to forever, Primrose De Luca," I whisper.

WHY THE FUCK IS THIS PARTY TAKING SO LONG? I WANT TO TAKE my bride back to the suite and do very marital things to her. I don't even care that she isn't a virgin anymore. He may have been her first, but I would be her last. Speaking of my bride, where the fuck is my angel?

I walk around the crowd of drunks as I look for Primrose, saying hi and wearing my best smile when I feel so irritated. I see Brixley dancing with Beckett. I push that fucker aside—I don't care if it's *their* thing. If anyone knows where my bride is, it's my pain-in-the-ass little sister.

She smiles. "Are you happy now?"

I grunt, spinning us around as I ask, "Where is my bride?"

"Oh." She breaks eye contact, the shit liar she is. "I don't know."

"You're a shit liar," I growl. "Tell me where she is."

Brixley's eyes shoot to the wide double doors, and I release her, stalking that way. I hear Brixley call after me, but I ignore her. I step into the hall, stalking to the wide-open balcony. Peeking behind a pillar, I see white tulle. My fists clench as I stalk that way. My hand twitches by my gun as I round the pillar, and what I see has murder flashing on my mind. That fucker came to our wedding and instead of being with me, I find her here with him.

"Vance." Primrose smiles up at me, reaching for me. I bat her hand away and hurt flashes across her face.

"Step away from my wife before I scatter your brains across the balcony and toss your body over it."

Fuck boy holds his hands up in surrender and backs away. I grab Primrose's hand, dragging her behind me, not caring that she keeps tripping over her own feet as she tries to keep up with my pace. "Vance, please slow down."

I spin on her, backing her into the wall next to the elevator. "Shut up," I growl. My body trembles with uncontrollable rage as the elevator dings. Roughly grabbing her arm, I pull her with me into the elevator, throwing my arm over her shoulders and pulling her into my side as I hit the button for the penthouse suite. Thankful she's silent as we travel up the floor, and yet, my anger doesn't die down as I pull her into the suite.

I push her down onto the bed, her back to me as I take my time unbuttoning the delicate buttons of her dress. My hands shake as I fight the urge to rip the dress but for some reason, I don't want to fuck something up she worked so hard on.

"Vance, can we talk about this?"

"Shut the fuck up for a moment," I mutter, pulling the dress off to reveal lace white panties underneath. I bite my fist hard as fuck. Closing my eyes, I try to calm myself down. It's futile. "It's one thing to let that fucker touch what's mine, take what's mine, but to come to our wedding, taking your time? Fuck no. I'm going to take what's mine now. And you're going to be my good little slut and spread those fucking legs for me, aren't you, Angel?" She nods as I slap the inside of her legs apart. She spreads them and I bend down. My eyes close as I sink my teeth into her peachy ass, leaving a bruising bite.

I slip my finger into the lace, ripping the seam until there is nothing but scraps at our feet. I undo my belt, letting my slacks fall to my knees as I position myself behind her. "Vance," she says almost desperately.

I squeeze my eyes shut. What am I doing? "You telling me you don't want me?" I ask.

"No, I do but—"

That's all I need to thrust deep inside her, something breaking and mixing with her hot juices. "Fuck, you're tight." I grunt, thrusting again.

I'm so blinded by anger, it takes me a moment to register her trembling body and the soft sniffles. My brow furrows as I pull myself out, looking down. "Oh, fuck," I hiss as blood coats my dick. "You..."

"Were a virgin? Yeah, Vance. If you would have listened, you'd know that." She sniffs, refusing to open her eyes.

"Fuck, baby girl."

She pushes back onto me. "No, you finish what you started. Don't go soft on me now." Her voice cracks.

"I can't." I pull out gently.

She flips over, caging her eyes with mine as her legs wrap around my waist. "Finish," she hisses.

I feel something in my chest snap as I slip back in, watching her body move back and forth with each thrust. Never breaking eye contact as she makes me pay for my arrogance. I pull out again, dropping to my knees in front of her. My hands gently slip up her thighs, parting her folds as I lay open-mouthed kisses on her soft, bloody flesh.

"What are you doing?" She whimpers.

"Apologizing," I murmur into her. Licking from tip to clit over and over again. I suck her bundle of nerves into my mouth, biting down lightly as she combs her fingers through my hair. And I let her.

She's so responsive, she comes quickly. The softest cries falling from her lips as she thrashes above me. I press more kisses to her inflamed skin before I rise. Pulling my pants up with me. She lays in blood-soaked sheets, her eyes closed with mascara stains on her cheeks. I grind my teeth, walking into the bathroom, starting a bath and pouring oils into it.

When I come back out, she hasn't moved. I cradle her small body in my arms, carrying her to the bathroom. Sitting her on the counter, I gently remove her heels. Not allowing myself to indulge in her lush curves. "Get in the bath. It'll take that pain away."

I turn to leave when her hand curls around my bicep, stopping me. I'm too numb to feel the burn of her touching me. "Are you happy now?" she asks.

I shake my head, walking backward slowly until she shuts the door.

What the fuck have I done?

11
PRIMROSE

He won't look at me. The room only had one bed last night and to my knowledge, he never slept in it. I don't know where he went. My first time didn't go as I imagined it would. No one told me it would hurt, that I would bleed. I've heard of popping cherries, but I never thought too much into it. My whole life—save for my father—I've been treated with kid gloves. Everyone has been gentle with me. The way Vance took me last night, how he said degrading things as he ripped my innocence to shreds, I... I liked it. But I'm not sure if he'll ever touch me again. He looked so horrified last night. Even though I wanted him to. I never expected hearts and roses from him. Not with how I can barely even touch him.

I look out the window of the car. Watching as palm trees and skies so blue they look like a painting pass. Vance woke me up early to get on a plane to take us to our honeymoon. Brixley and Amiyah stole my suitcase and replaced it with several others I've never seen in my life. Makes me nervous as to what will be in there, but it was too late to find out.

"Vance," I say softly. He doesn't budge from his phone. "Vance," I try again. "Look at me." He does. Eyes dark, jaw tight. "About last night..."

"I don't think we should talk about it right now."

"Well, thankfully, that's my decision to make. I know Cooper makes you angry, and as you now know, you have no reason to be. I feel like I have to explain the situation anyways. Cooper needed a tutor, I wanted extra money. So, I tutored him last semester. We became friends, but that's all it ever was. He lives very close to my childhood home, that's why he took me home for summer break. Now, as for last night, he was telling me bye. He's transferring."

Vance looks to his lap, sighing. "I'm—"

I hold up a hand. "Don't apologize. I personally don't want to hear it. I'm done being a victim and I'm done allowing people to tell me what to do. If you want to touch me, you ask. I will continue to work with you on physical touch but any trust we have built is gone. I don't care if I liked it. I may be your wife now, but I'm not your property to do whatever you want with." I take a deep breath. "Now, how long is this honeymoon?"

"Need to be back before the new semester starts." I nod. "Are you going to allow me to build our trust back?" he asks. A little out of character for him.

"Very slowly," I mumble.

VANCE OPENS THE DOOR TO THE SMALL CONDO ON A PRIVATE beach. I immediately take in the modern look, not loving it. I like antique things. Something with a story and character.

These condos have been redone to provide luxury—not so sure about comfort yet.

A man in a colorful Hawaii-print shirt brings our luggage in on a cart and heads down the hallway. I walk through the open-floor plan to the sliding back doors that open to a pool and hot tub on a wooden deck that overlooks the ocean. There are blue and red striped lounge chairs. Tables with matching umbrellas. I step back inside to catch Vance speaking in fluent Italian on the phone as he paces the kitchen. I walk down the hall, noticing only one door, and my stomach sinks as I come to the only room with one bed. It's a big bed, don't get me wrong, but why would he not get a condo with two rooms?

I close the door, locking it as I walk over to my new suitcases. I open one, and—surprise, surprise—it's filled with skimpy lingerie and anal beads. I shake my head as I open the next one. Bathing suits in all colors, all thong based, but hey, they got me some sunblock and cover-ups. I pull out a red thong swimsuit bottom, twirling it around my finger as I do a three-way video call with my *friends*.

"Love!" Amiyah sings into the phone.

"She must have looked in her special suitcases," Brixley says in greeting.

"What is this?" I hold up the red scrap of material.

"Oh, I picked that one out. It's so hot," Amiyah replies, smiling her big white smile.

I narrow my eyes at them both. "You both know I don't wear things like this."

"Yeah, but you're hot, Prim. Time for you to see that," Brixley responds, petting Samson. I wanted to bring him with us, but Brix offered to keep him. Wish I would have declined that offer so I could have him with me for comfort.

"How was last night? I bet his di—"

"Eww!" Brixley screams. "That's my brother, Miya!"

My smile falls and they both frown with me. "What is it, love?" Amiyah asks.

I look away, nibbling on my lip. And then, I begin. I tell them everything from last night. Not leaving anything out, including how I liked the nature of it just not the way it was conducted. By the end, I'm breathing hard, and both of my friends are silent with rage. Maybe sadness? I have no clue.

"He didn't rape you?" Brixley asks, breaking the silence.

I shake my head. "No, just didn't give me the chance to explain that I was a virgin."

"Where does this leave you, babe? Do you want out of the relationship?" Amiyah asks.

"I never said I wanted in it." *A lie.*

"Yeah, but we could all see it even when you both couldn't." I stay quiet, pondering that. She's right, I just wasn't aware anyone was paying attention.

"Here is some advice you didn't ask for," Amiyah begins. "Every article of clothing in your suitcase is designed to bring a man to his knees. I want you to use that as a form of torture."

I scoff. "I have scars on my back and face, no one is tortured by my looks." *Except maybe me.*

"So, so naïve, Primrose," Brixley bristles. "Put that swimsuit on and walk out, and see how much you are desired. Know your fucking worth. Scars or not, you're gorgeous."

"Exactly. And send pics." Amiyah winks.

I blow a kiss to them in goodbye and sigh. There is a knock on the door, and I jump slightly. "Everything okay in there?" Vance asks.

"Yeah." I look down at the red swimsuit. "Just changing."

THE TOP WRAPS AROUND MY NECK, PUSHING MY GIRLS TOGETHER, and I'm honestly afraid they will fall out. The bottoms rise high on my hips and expose more than I ever would of my ass. Even my panties of choice are rated PG-13. I turn in the mirror; my ass is nice, though. Shaking my head, I grab a pair of flip-flops and slide them on my feet. Placing my sunglasses on my face as I fix my big, floppy hat. With one quick look in the mirror, I take a deep breath and walk out. My eyes meet his immediately, and he pauses his stride, phone placed at his ear as his eyes rake over me.

"I'll call you back," he says in a thick voice that makes me shiver, but I don't have time for that. I walk to the sliding back doors, walk across the patio, and open the gate that leads to the beach.

"Where are you going?" I can hear his voice closer to me than it should be, but I ignore him. "Angel." He cups my elbow and I yank it away.

"I told you in the car the new terms. I don't have to answer you, Vance."

He combs his hands through his longish hair. "I'm not a patient man, Primrose. And I expect you to at least tell me where you're going."

"Obviously, the beach. Where else could I go?"

"Dressed like that?" His eyes rake back down me again and a smirk breaks over his lips. "To our bed."

"You wish," I sass. Turning around and continuing my journey.

"You could have invited me," he says, a little farther away now.

"You're a grown man. Do what you want."

I kick my flip-flips off, tossing my hat and glasses to the sand, and walk into the shockingly frigid water. Once the water is waist deep, I dive in. I love the way the water molds to me. So crisp and weightless. I emerge from the water, pushing my hair back out of my face as I walk up to the shore. I wipe my eyes when a strong hand grips my throat and pulls me into a hard body.

"You think you're going to walk around, teasing me with your peachy ass, and I'm not going to touch you?" he asks over my lips.

"Yes." *Confidence, not breathless, Primrose.*

"Nah, baby girl. You may think I don't own this," his free hand grips my ass in his big palm, squeezing, "but I do." He trails his tongue over my lips, biting down on the bottom one.

I try to pull away but his hand around my throat tightens. He rubs his hard, thick length over my stomach. "I said—"

"I heard you, Angel, doesn't mean I'm going to listen."

I stomp my foot on his bare one. Shouldn't have taken his shoes off. He loosens his grip and I pull away. "You will this time, Vance." I grab my things and walk back up to the condo. A huge smile on my face.

I'm giving him hell.

I blow out a breath as I look down at the *sleep clothes* I must choose from. Lace and silk, they didn't care that I prefer cotton, obviously. I grab a dark pink silk shirt that is cropped with black lace and matching tiny shorts, slipping them on in the bathroom. We ordered in and I grabbed a quick shower, then blow-dried my hair which always takes so long my arm grows tired by the end of it. I grab my bag and begin my face routine, focusing heavily on the scar. It's weird, when I'm with Vance I almost forget it's there, but when looking in the mirror, it's hard not to notice it. Once I'm done, I open the connecting bathroom door.

Vance lays out on the bed in sweats with his inked chest bare. He holds the phone up as he speaks to the screen. I take the chance to admire him. How his thick raven hair is a perfect mess. Jawline sharp and dusted in hair that trails around his full lips. His dark, almost black eyes surrounded by thick lashes and strong eyebrows. His tan skin is covered in dark, sinister tattoos. Shoulders big and broad with veiny arms.

My eyes snap back to his face as he speaks, "No, I want that property. It's isolated and away from the city, it'll be the perfect place to make and store cocaine." He has his AirPods in, so I don't hear the person's response. "Nah, no meth, we're not selling that shit." A pause and then, "Don't give a fuck, we're not pushing it." His eyes connect with mine over the phone, and he winks. It shoots straight through me, curling at my toes. I blush as I walk over to my only bag I packed that made it on the trip. I grab my current read and head out of the room. I take a seat on the striped, blue lounge chair and get lost between the pages of a western outlaw romance.

"Are you reading outlaw porn, Angel?"

I startle as a blush crawls up my cheeks. "It's not porn," I say defensively.

Vance sits on the end of the lounge, marker box in hand. "No?" He raises his eyebrows. "Let me see it then."

I pull the book protectively against my chest. "No."

He laughs. "Is that what you want? Me to dress up like a cowboy and fuck you in a field under a stary night?"

I laugh. "No way. That seems nice, but in reality, chiggers would eat us alive, not to mention mosquitoes."

Vance licks his lips, eyes falling to my exposed legs. "Yeah. You ready to color on me or would you like to skip that tonight?"

I sit my book down, rising. "Go ahead and lay back, I'll pull a chair up so I can color on your arm," I say as I begin to go grab a chair.

Vance grabs my hand, stopping me. I look down, confused. "I want you to color my neck instead."

"Really?" I ask, shocked. I've made it to his elbow so far, the neck is quite a jump.

"Yeah. You'll have to sit on my lap, though, your tiny arms won't reach from a chair."

A lie. We both know it but neither of us speak a word about it. "Okay."

Vance lays on his back, eyes staring up at the star-covered sky. Gently, I crawl onto his lap, sitting my box of markers on his chest. "Is this okay?" I ask.

"Yeah, baby girl," he says, closing his eyes.

I take out my neon colors, starting with the wolf's eyes. Maybe it's wrong, but I make them blue like my own. They look like glaciers, ready to melt. I begin softly coloring the wolf's teeth. The tops a deep green fading to pink. I zone in on coloring his dark-inked skin into a work of bright, colorful art. Like a watercolor tattoo.

His skin is warm under my touch, his breath fanning over my cheek as I try to focus, but it's impossible. Every inch of our bodies touching feels like fire. I move slightly, moving over the thick length beneath his sweats, hitting my sensitive spot. I feel his finger tracing the lace on the collar of my silk sleep shirt. Teasing the valley of my breasts before he moves it back over the swell, driving me mad.

"My turn," he whispers. Putting the box of markers on the ground next to us and flipping me over so I'm under him. He grabs a black marker, his free hand pushing my shirt up to free my breasts. The breeze from the sea causing my nipples to perk up. He bites the cap off with his teeth, spitting the cap to the side.

Why is that so hot?

His eyes are like fire as he stares down at me, before pressing the marker to my skin and sliding it down between my breasts. His free hand runs over my collarbone as he draws, sliding up to my lips and pressing down on the bottom until I'm forced to open for him. He runs his thumb over my tongue. I stare wide-eyed at him as his finger slips from my tongue and goes to my scar, all while never breaking focus from his drawing. He drops the marker, looking down at me. Leaning down he runs his lips over the scar and my eyes close.

"Do you trust me?" he asks.

"I think we established that I don't."

"What if I wanted to tattoo what I just drew, would you let me? Without knowing what it is?" There is a challenge in his voice. And I can't help but want to accept it.

"Okay," I whisper.

He smirks, walking inside as bright lights come on, illuminating the back patio. It's a fight not to peek at what's drawn on my skin, but I somehow manage. He comes back out, tattoo gun case in hand. "Glad I brought this with me," he says, pulling up a chair next to me.

"I didn't even know they came cordless," I breathe as he wipes down my skin. "Wait, did you just wipe the drawling away?"

He taps his head. "I got it memorized, don't worry."

Like a true man, he only answers one out of two questions. I close my eyes as he places the needle to my sternum and, oh my freaking god, does it hurt. Such a sensitive area, but I stay as still as I can. It only takes close to an hour but by the time he's done, my body is pumping with adrenalin. He teases my nipples with a pinch of his fingers, somehow making me come alive with a simple touch.

With strong hands he lifts me in his arms, walking us inside. I keep my hands to my sides, respecting his boundaries even if he doesn't respect mine.

He drops me on the bed, pressing a button as a mirror opens up on the ceiling, showing me my lust-filled gaze and the predator beside me.

"We rectify this now. You're going to watch as I fuck you the right way."

I shake my head, turning my head to face him. "I don't want to see myself."

He tilts his head. "Why not?"

I rise onto my knees, resting on my calves as I stare down. "Because I'm ugly, this scar is hideous, and I refuse to look at it."

Vance reaches in his sweatpants pocket, pulling out a knife. It all happens so fast I don't even have time to gasp as he slices it down his face, on the exact spot and side as my scar. Tossing the knife he says, "Am I ugly now? Does this," he points to his bleeding face as I stare wide-eyed, "take away and define all that I am?" He shakes his head. "No, now come here." He pulls me by my throat, smashing his lips to mine and forcing his tongue into my mouth. His other hand slips into my shorts, two fingers fucking me with no mercy as he sucks on my tongue. He breaks away, breaths heavy as he looks between both of my eyes. "Lay on the bed, wrist together above your head."

I follow the orders due to my lack of sanity, and the lust. As I wait for him, I stare at the single black rose, the thorned stem, and his name scripted underneath it. *Did he just mark me, with his own name?* He positions his body over mine, blocking my view. Black duct tape in his hands as he leans over, wrapping my wrists together. "Keep them there," he commands, placing a strip of tape over my lips. He looks down at me and smirks. "In case you want to tell me no."

I watch in the mirror above me as he pulls his sweats off and then my eyes are back on him. His angry length as he strokes it harshly, squeezing his head roughly. I want a better look at it, but he blocks my view by climbing back on top of me, ripping my shorts down my legs. He rubs his length against my folds, watching with the look of an addict. My cheeks flush when I hear the wetness of my want for him. For whatever sinister intent he has planned for me. "Don't give a fuck whether or not you're on birth control, Angel. Going to fuck you long and hard. And I'm going to feel this tight pussy grip every inch of me raw and then I'll paint your insides with my cum. How does that sound?" My back arches from his words alone.

He trails a single finger over my hip, teasing my entrance with his tip. I wish he'd put me out of my torture. He chuckles, pinching my nipple hard and I moan, arching into his touch. He lights every nerve ending on fire with one touch. He pushes into me slowly and unlike our wedding night, it doesn't hurt too much. He closes his eyes, tilting his head back and moaning as he sinks in farther, stretching me wide to accommodate his thick, long length. His moan is... the sexiest form of Vance I've seen so far.

Finally, he sinks all the way in, filling me so fully I want to grind against him. His eyes flash open and he leans over me, gripping my wrists in one hand as his chest plasters to mine, and then he's moving and, oh my god, this is sex? I moan as his lips kiss my neck, his wound dripping blood on me as his teeth nip at my throat like an animal as he tears into the flesh there. I know he's broke skin, but I don't care.

"Watch yourself in the mirror, Angel."

I do, looking up and seeing my bound wrists, my taped mouth, eyes lust-filled and glassy, cheeks a rosy pink and flushed as he moves deep inside me. His back muscles work, his strong tatted arms flexing, along with his ass muscles as he thrusts in and out of me.

"Look how fucking hot you are, my little incubus. Watch as your body leaks with sex appeal, how mine feasts off of it," he rasps, kissing my cheek. "You're so fucking sexy, Primrose De Luca, I can't fucking think straight when I'm around you." He rises, hooking my legs to his hips and thrusting in hard. "You're strangling my cock, wife." He grunts, before ripping the tape off my mouth and growls, "Now scream my fucking name, let the whole island know who owns this tight little body, let them know who your husband is."

I cry out as he pounds inside of me, screaming his name with his thumb working my tight bundle of nerves until I'm thrashing. My bound hands twist into the sheets as tears leak from my eyes, the emotions of having my first earth-shattering orgasm taking hold of me. It's so intense, my vision goes blurry as I hear him moan, stiffening and letting hot liquid fill my insides.

He catches his breath as he rubs the cum inside me,

massaging it into my walls. "Such a good little wife," he praises. Grabbing his knife, he cuts the tape from my wrists and climbs off of me. His phone rings and he curses, grabbing it and walking out to speak.

And me? I'm so spent I fall asleep exactly as he left me.

12
VANCE

IN ANOTHER LIFE, I would be a millionaire who gets to stay home buried in his wife until he was ready to leave. *Which would be never.* I've had several sexual partners, their gender never important. After the abuse of my aunt, I was down to erase any trace of her. I had no clue what I was into, only that they had to be bound. I did make the mistake of not bounding one, just to see, and well, I attacked her. Fucked-up situation my dad had to handle. But Primrose? A whole new experience. Sex has always been... a simple need I experience sometimes and when my hand doesn't work, I seek it out, but with my wife, it's an addiction.

Her lush, curvy body. Her expressive little doe eyes, her light moans and cries. She lights up under my touch like never before, and I actually want her to touch me, but I don't want to fucking hurt her. Touch is a trigger, we have a long way to go, but for now, holding her hand and allowing her to color my tattoos is okay.

"You're not listening," my annoying cousin says.

I sigh. "We discussed this last night. Burn the fucking letters and don't call me while I'm on my honeymoon.

Probably just the Russian Bratva. And besides, my father is still the head, so why are you bothering me with this?"

"He said it involves your wife, so, it's your problem."

"That shit can wait. I'm on an isolated island, doubt they can get here." I click End Call on my phone and place it in the pocket of my jeans.

I walk inside and see Primrose in the kitchen, her hair down. A light, long violet-colored skirt and a lace crop top that has skinny straps wrapped around her curves. She walks to the living room, grabbing her big floppy hat. She avoids the mirror completely and I have an urge to grab her neck and force her to look at herself. My own hand touches the sharp sting of the cut on my face. It'll leave a scar, not as deep as I would have liked—not that I was thinking straight when I did it. I was angry at her response. I had to calm myself down, so I didn't take her savagely again. We'll slowly move on to that as we get more comfortable.

"Ready?" I ask, checking my notifications to see our Uber has arrived.

She nods, throwing her sunglasses on and draping her purse over her shoulder. "Where are we going, exactly?"

"Brunch." I open the door for her, shutting it behind us as I follow her to the car.

The driver is young, taking his job way too seriously as he explains there are complimentary snacks and water by our feet. He looks in the rearview mirror, eyes zeroing in on my wife as I narrow mine on him. "You are very pretty, miss."

"Eyes on the road," I snap, throwing my arm around my angel and pulling her closer. "Fucker," I mumble under my breath. Leaning into her ear, I whisper, "Seems my mark on your neck isn't going to cut it."

She giggles, and I smile. She likes my caveman tendencies even if she pretends to be immune to them. "I think he's just trying to get a nice tip," she whispers back.

I shake my head, lips positioned at the side of her head. "Nah, he wanted to feel us out, see if you belong to me or if you're free game."

The car pulls up to a beach house restaurant. It looks like anything but a high-class restaurant, but I had to book this place when I made the reservations for our condo months ago. I open the door for Primrose, allowing her to walk a bit ahead of me before I shove my head back in the car. "Instead of a tip, I'm going to allow you to keep your eyes instead of taking them as collateral for looking at what's mine."

The driver's eyes widen and his mouth opens and closes like a fish out of water. I slam the door, walking up behind Primrose and grabbing her hand. She looks down at our joined hands, a tiny smile on her face as she looks up to me behind dark shades. "Did you tip him nicely?"

I smirk. "I sure did."

I open the door to the restaurant. The place looks like a ship on the inside, lots of old boards and anchors, fishnet hanging from the ceiling. "Welcome to Rusty Anchors, do you have a reservation?" the host asks, his uniform absolutely absurd. A sailor suit. Crazy I had to put down a thousand-dollar deposit just to hold my spot here.

"Yeah, two for De Luca."

The host scans his computer, eyes narrowed and concentrated. "Oh, yes. You have the deck view. Right this way."

We walk through the restaurant, people who reek of rich perfume and timeshares littered everywhere. We follow him out onto the deck, to the table right in front of the ocean.

"Oh," Primrose says, looking over the ocean. Her face lights up and she takes her hat and sunglasses off, placing them on the table next to her. She smiles at some seals as they make weird fucking noises at one another. And that right there, the look of pure happiness on her face, is why spending that thousand dollars isn't shit. Her light hair blows with the sea breeze, the sun highlighting the small specks of freckles scattering over her nose and under her eyes. She's been free of makeup for a while now, saved for our wedding day. She used to never wear makeup, but since the Devlin incident, I haven't seen her in public without it. Doesn't help that she doesn't have any now—since I threw it away. But let's be fucking real here, she doesn't need it. I love how obsession just sneaks up on you. Like a snake bite, the venom sinking into your bloodstream before you even know you've been bitten.

The waiter comes up to us, another fucking man wearing a ridiculous-ass sailor outfit. "What can I get you?"

"I'll take a water," I say, looking to my wife.

"Can I have a strawberry mimosa, please?" She smiles, making that bastard waiter's eyes twinkle and his cheeks tint.

"Sure, I'll get those out to you soon."

"Hey," I say. She looks over to me, still smiling. "Do you like blood on your hands?"

She blinks once. "What?"

I lean over the table so she can hear me, "Every time you smile, these fuckers get the wrong idea. I'm going to start cutting out eyes and chopping off hands."

She swallows. "I'm just being polite."

"I know that, but they don't. You smile and they think

they have a chance. We both know I'm not a patient man. So, keep your smiles for me only."

She shakes her head. "You're insane."

I nod. "Only for you, *wife*."

PRIMROSE'S CHEEKS ARE FLUSHED, HER EYES GLASSY AS SHE SIPS another mimosa. "They taste just like juice." She giggles.

"Hate to break it to you, Angel, but you're drunk."

She laughs. "I think I would know."

I shake my head. "I don't think you would." I hold my hand out, before saying, "Come on, let's get out of here."

She takes my hand but pauses. "Can we swim with the dolphins?"

"Did your friends pack you an appropriate swimsuit?" I arch an eyebrow.

She pouts. "No."

"Then no."

She pulls on my hand, making me stop. "But, Vance, I want to. Besides," she holds up her left finger, showing off her vintage diamond wedding ring, "this right here proves I belong to you. And so what if people look." She comes closer, wrapping her arms around my neck, I flinch only slightly. She bats those thick lashes at me, those doe eyes wide and pleading. "I'm going home with you." She kisses the corner of my lips. "So let them stare, it doesn't matter at the end of the day."

Oh, she's good.

I sigh. "You trying to work your succubus magic on me, Angel?"

She nods, kissing me sweetly, and I take the opportunity to deepen the kiss, growling as I pull away. *God fucking dammit.* "Let's go," I snap.

"Back to the condo?" she asks, sadly.

"Yeah, to get swimsuits and see the fucking dolphins. You know they're vile creatures, right?"

"Yes," she says happily. "But I have a thing for vile creatures."

You have no fucking idea how true that is, Angel.

Primrose giggles as a dolphin laughs with her. I, however, am on the phone, managing the new club we are opening. I want to be swimming with my wife—couldn't care less about the dolphins—but I'm not. "I don't fucking care," I say harshly into the phone, getting ready to end the call on Daddy dearest.

"Son."

"I'm on my fucking honeymoon," I growl. "I'm throwing this fucking phone into the ocean, good luck getting a hold of me."

I hear him go to speak but I launch the phone into the dark depths of the water. *Good riddance.*

"Honey." I pause, looking down at my half-drunk, giggling wife in a life jacket as she pets a dolphin. I raise my eyebrows at her pet name. "Why did you just throw your phone in the ocean?" she asks.

"Get out of the water," I say, running my hands through my hair.

"Bye, Barron." *Even the fucking dolphin is male.*

I hold the towel open for her as she pulls her life jacket off. "You hungry?"

She yawns, nodding. "Yeah, but can you have dinner delivered? I want to get into the hot tub."

"The hot tub, huh?" She nods. "We can arrange that."

Now that my phone is gone, the only thing I have to focus on is my wife. Finally.

13
PRIMROSE

I LAY my head back on the stone of the hot tub, staring up at the sunset. I've spent most of the rest of the day in the water, Vance inside doing whatever mafia princes do. Looked like computer work. I thought when he threw his phone into the ocean he would have more time for me, but it would seem like his judgment has gotten the better of him. We had Chinese takeout for dinner. The mimosa haze I was in wore off by the afternoon, making me a little tired but I've powered through it.

I sigh into the hot, steaming water, my mind flashing back to last night. How he took me slow and hard. It was definitely more intimate than the first time, but I missed the roughness, the degradation. But I'm not sure how to bring something up like that. How do I confess that when I can't even say the word cock?

And I have no idea how to react to him cutting his perfect face, just to show me how ridiculous I was being. It was such a sweet, yet crazy thing to do. He was so unhinged, unbothered about baring his face open for me.

It left me feeling a bit vulnerable.

I'm thankful that I am in fact on birth control—for menstrual reasons—because I'm so not ready for a child right now. Especially as we still try to navigate our lives with one another. I'm still not sure if it will work out. I know that divorce is not an option, but him taking a mistress is. My heart stings at the thought of him with another.

The back door opens, and I turn my head to watch Vance walk out. His big frame eats up the distance between us. His unholy tattoos flexing with each movement. The way his abs ripple, and contract makes me want to sink beneath the warm surface. He rests his towel on the seat close by, kicking his slides off. My eyes lower as he sinks into the tub across from me, stretching his arms across the rock edge as he watches me. His leg wraps in mine, tangling us together.

"Did you get your work done?" I ask.

"I don't want to talk about work." He hooks his legs around my thighs, tugging. "Come here." He pulls me onto his lap, looking down at my black bikini top. He leans over, licking the drops of water from the swells that bob in the water. I moan, my hands going to his hair, and he pauses, biting down harshly, and I lift them. "Put your arms behind your back."

I do, of course I do. I'm fucking gone to lust for this man. He unhooks the chain from around his neck, then proceeds to twist it tightly around my wrists.

"When will I be able to touch you?" I ask. I want to touch him... everywhere. Place gentle kisses to his covered-in-sin skin.

He shakes his head. "I don't know, baby girl. But I want to keep you safe."

"From what?" I ask as he unties the top of my bikini, baring hard rose-pink nipples to him.

"From myself. Touching me while we fuck, it's not a good idea."

"Why?" I arch toward him as he sucks one nipple into his mouth, distracting me. His hand wraps in my hair, tugging sharply as I arch further. Small moans breaking free as he sucks, nips, and licks my breast. I feel a tingle in my core, and I have the urge to move against him.

"Such a dirty slut for me, aren't you, Angel?"

"Yes." I moan, giving in to the need to grind against him.

He chuckles into my breast, then places a kiss between them. "You like that, don't you?"

"Like what?" I say breathlessly.

"When I call you a slut."

My cheeks go hot, and I grind harder. He abruptly lifts us and I whine in disappointment. He lays me on the lounge on my stomach, pulling my bottoms off. "On your knees, face in the pillow," he commands. I do as he says, struggling without my arms. "Fuck, look at you," he rasps as I feel him crawl behind me.

I feel his hot breath fall on my heat and then I feel his tongue there. Lapping up my juices, and it's something I've never felt before. It feels dirty in the most delicious way.

"Vance," I moan into the lounge cushion.

I feel his hands on my ass, slowly spreading me as his tongue moves up and teases my hole. I gasp, my entire body heating in embarrassment. "Relax," he whispers into me, biting down on the thick flesh of my ass. I do, slowly. He works me there, and it doesn't feel strange like I thought it would. It feels... amazing. I feel his tongue inside me, and my knees begin to buckle, but his hand cuffs my pussy, holding me up. His fingers start working me there as his mouth works my ass. I moan, thrashing. I feel like I'm going to explode. His mouth leaves me, before a finger enters me. I explode, convulsing into the lounge as my head spins in ecstasy.

It takes my body a minute to calm down, him slowly stroking my skin doesn't help, but finally I stop twitching. And he allows me to drop. He unhooks my hands and I turn over to face him. "I want to do that for you."

"Do what, Angel?"

"I want to... I want to put you in my mouth and taste you, please."

His eyes shine and he looks away quickly. "That's not in our cards."

I sit up quickly. "Why? What happened to you?"

"I don't want to talk about it."

I cross my arms, feeling sad for him and not knowing why. "Well, I think we should."

"I said no," he snaps, and I flinch away from him.

"I'm just trying to help," I say quietly.

"Well, stop. This is all I have to offer, Primrose. Get used to it."

"Vance—"

"I'm leaving." He grabs his towel, tying it around his waist.

I quickly get up, following after him. "Wait, where are you going?" I follow him into the room.

"Away from this conversation." He slams the door of the bathroom in my face.

I sit on the bed as I listen to him shower and then rise before he comes out, freshly dressed in dark jeans and a black V-neck. "Where are you going?" I ask again.

"Out." He grabs his cigarettes and wallet, stuffing them into his pockets.

"If you warm another bed, don't come back to ours."

"Noted." And then he's gone and something in my chest cracks a little.

THE BED IS EMPTY AND THERE IS NO HARSH ITALIAN COMING FROM outside of the room. Which is how I wake up often to him on the phone. Sighing, I sit up on the bed. *Fine.* I get up, getting ready for the day. I don't have to do everything with him. I can make my own memories. It's been that way most of my life anyway. I grab a banana and container for my seashell collection from the kitchen and head to the beach. The wind is harsh as I lay the beach blanket out. I sit, batting my wild strands out of my face as I watch the sun rise over the crashing waves. The sky is pink and orange, something so beautiful it's almost unimaginable. I can hear the birds chirping and I close my eyes as I allow the peace of the morning to consume me.

I rise, walking along the beach and picking up seashells. I came to the beach once when I was younger, but it was for a wedding and Father wouldn't allow me to get dirty or play with the other kids. I remember longing to be like the other children, their pants rolled to their knees as they jumped in the waves. I wondered how the sand felt between their toes. But now I don't have to. Because I'm free to do so.

Momma would love it here. Every time she enters my mind, a crippling pain breaks through my chest, almost bringing me to my knees. The wind whips my hair in my face as I take a seat on the blanket again. "Momma?" It feels silly, but I need to talk to her. "I'm so lost. This man is... he's confusing." I laugh to myself. "But I think I really like him, and maybe, he likes me. I mean, he's possessive, but is it maybe because he looks at me as a possession, like Father?" I shake my head. "I don't know, Momma." *This is stupid, she can't hear me.* "Am I an idiot for falling for him?" I wait for an answer, a sign. Holding my breath, but it never comes.

I grab my things, ordering an Uber as I make my way to the condo. It's not empty this time, but I don't bother going to where I can hear him. I drop my beach stuff and grab my bag, not bothering with a hat today. I don't feel like hiding from the world right now. I hurry down to the waiting car and don't look back to see if he tried to catch me. *He didn't come back last night.*

He's not your problem anymore.

14
VANCE

I watch her climb into the car, leaving without saying goodbye. *God dammit.* I spent last night drowning my memories in a bottle of whiskey as I walked the beach like some loser. I couldn't call and tell her that because my phone is sleeping with the fishes. When she asked if she could taste me, I almost came in my fucking pants, but I couldn't allow her to. I didn't want to fucking snap her neck if Lucia's image flashed in my mind while she was doing it.

I just want to be normal.

I walk back into the house and grab my computer, ordering an Uber to the nearest phone shop. I wasn't going to but not having a way to communicate with my angel just won't work. So, I grab my wallet and head out.

A few hours later, I have a new phone and head back to the condo. She's finally back, sitting on the couch curled up with a book. I pause in front of her and she lifts an eyebrow.

"Hi," I say. She rolls her eyes, scoffing. "I didn't sleep with anyone else," I rush to tell her. *And why am I even explaining myself to her?*

She sets her book down and looks up to me. "Where were you?"

"Walking on the beach, getting drunk."

She nods. "The only way you and I can be together is if you're honest with me. You need to tell me what happened to you so that I can understand why I can't touch you."

I grip my hair in my fist. "Fine, but don't you dare look at me with pity once I tell you. You can never unlearn it and it's going to fuck with you."

"Whatever demons you face I will conquer," she says confidently.

Yeah, we'll see.

I take a deep breath and begin.

Age Nine

My door creaks open and I curse under my breath. "Vance." I used to find her voice sweet but now I get sick every time I hear it. "It's time to play."

I squeeze my eyes shut, hoping maybe tonight she'll just go find her husband. She pulls the covers back. I look up as she smiles down at me. "Why are you hiding, sweetie?" she asks as if she's hurt by that. I don't say anything, I just keep my eyes trained on hers, my mouth closed. She shrugs. "I used to do the same when my brother's best friend came over, but between you and I, we never loved each other like you and I do. It's not the same thing."

I swallow as she moves under the covers with me. Her hands find my pajama pants and she tugs them down. I close my eyes and swallow down the need to cry. Mafia men don't cry. We are not weak. Her hand glides over me and I wield the stupid thing to not react to her, but it does. I can't control it. I don't like this, but still, I always get hard even though I'm silently screaming inside for help. I hear her moan and my stomach sours, and I turn my head away, pressing it into the pillow as far as I can.

"We are going to try something new this time. I think you'll like it."

She moves down and my eyes shoot open, staring at the wall as I feel her place her mouth over me. She moans and my eyes swell with tears but I don't let them fall. I grit my teeth as she licks me. Don't come, I chant to myself over and over again but my body doesn't listen. I come. My mind zoning her and the entire situation out. Acting as if it's not happening.

Present

I stare at my feet, waiting for her response, but it never comes. I look up to see her looking at her hands, pulling on the fabric of her dress. Is she judging me now? Does she find me as repulsive as I find myself? Can she see my whole flirty personality is a front, except when it comes to her?

"Did you ever tell anyone?" she asks.

"No." I swallow.

She nods, understanding me on some level. I've seen the old scars on her back. "When was the last time?"

"When I was fourteen and put a gun to her head."

"Good," she whispers, rising.

"Where are you going?" *Why is there a desperation in my voice?*

"To get my markers. Take your shirt off, husband."

I smile, to make her feel more comfortable even though I'm still feeling the aftermath of my confession. I slip my shirt off as she comes back in. I lay back on the couch as she sits beside me, eyes roving over my body as if I'm a work of art she wants to caress. *I wish she could.*

She begins coloring the demon war zone on my chest. "Did you know," she begins. "There is only one letter in the alphabet that doesn't appear in any of the American states —Q. Weird, huh?"

I relax a little more into the couch, listening to her random facts that are oddly calming for some reason. "I never thought about it."

"Why would you? It's not something we think about. Also, another thing we've never thought of. Ketchup used to be sold as indigestion medicine."

"Are tomatoes not harsh on stomach acid?" I ask.

"Exactly," she says, working her way down to my devil tattoo. I take a deep breath as she places the marker there, coloring softly. "Fewer children are born on Saturdays."

I laugh. "The fuck am I supposed to do with that information?"

She looks up, grinning. "Nothing, but look. I finished coloring the devil and you didn't even flinch."

I look down with a furrowed brow. It is done, and she's right, it didn't bother me. Figured it would since it was so close to my cock.

I look back at her. "Let's get some sleep, Angel. I've been up twenty-four hours."

She smiles, holding her hand out, and I take it. Allowing her to pull me to bed.

15
PRIMROSE

We walk through the front door of Vance's home. Sadly, the honeymoon couldn't last forever, but I wish it could have. We spent the last week touring the town, seeing exotic fish aquariums and eating so much, I'm sure I've gained twenty pounds. But at night, he'd whisper dirty things in my ear as I was bound with whatever he could get his hands on and took no mercy on my body.

But all dreams must come to an end.

Adriano stands in the living room, staring down at his phone. I sigh at the sight of him. My keeper.

"Lovebirds are back, I see," he says.

"Why are in you in my house?" Vance clips out.

"Just checking the perimeters."

"I have people for that." Vance narrows his eyes and Adriano shifts.

"I just wanted to make sure it was completely safe before you came home, is all."

Silence, and then, "Well, is it?"

Adriano nods. "It is."

Vance's jaw tics. "Then get the hell out."

"Will do, sir."

Adriano hurries to the door and quickly leaves. "Idiot," Vance mumbles under his breath.

Vance grabs two of my suitcases, carrying them upstairs. He turns to his room, and I stop on the threshold. "What are you doing?"

"Putting your stuff in our room."

"Our room?"

He tosses the suitcases down, turning to look at me. "We've been sharing a bed for weeks, I'm not about to sleep alone now."

"You didn't even ask if that is what I want."

"You haven't woken up screaming in your sleep since we've shared a bed. I don't have to ask if that's what you want, it's what you need."

I bite my lip as he walks back downstairs. It's true, I haven't, but I didn't think it had anything to do with him and everything to do with me moving on in life. I guess it could be both. No need to allow him to win everything. He comes back up the stairs and I point my thumb to my old room. "I just need to get my stuff."

He shakes his head. "No need. Already had everything moved over here. That is your sewing room now."

"Oh." I purse my lips, then walk into *our* bedroom and it's every bit of darkness I expected from him. Black silk bedding on a giant bed that sits low to the ground. Lights come from the fabric frame under it. Dark floors and charcoal gray walls. Long black drapes hang from the windows. A giant stone fireplace rests on the wall ahead of the bed, two imposing doors on either side. The walls are bare. The room tidy as if it's nothing more than a guest room. There is nothing personal lingering on the tops of the drawers or bedside tables.

I walk to one door, my mouth dropping open at the first room I find—the bathroom. Gold and black marble countertops. A huge mirror with touch screen something, I don't even know. I continue my way and push the last door open. The entire room is in black tile, showerheads hang from the roof and along the walls. In the middle is a huge stone bath with a rainfall showerhead above it. The whole freaking room is a shower. "Whoa."

"Do with the house what you like," Vance says from behind me, making me jump.

"I'm not going to change your home."

He shrugs. "It's our home now. Do whatever you want. Not like I give a fuck."

"I think your home is beautiful. Like the castle in *Beauty and the Beast*."

"Fitting," he muses as I hear his footsteps walk away.

I walk back out to the room to see Vance tossing cards on the bed. He points to a black card. "That's our joint account." He motions to another card one that looks like it may be made of gold. "Your account." He points to the next. "New driver's license, and passport."

I hold up my hand. "First of all, that's illegal," I motion to my passport and driver's license. "Second of all, I don't have an account worthy of a gold card, and I don't want your money." I cross my arms over my chest.

"Personally, I don't give a fuck, baby girl. You have my last name, anything that is mine is yours." He looks up to me, thinking. "We need to get you a car."

I throw my hands up. "There is no reason for me to have one, you're with me all the time."

He smiles. "As much as it kills me, you will have to do things on your own eventually."

"You mean, me and Adriano," I mumble.

"Unless he has somehow offended or hurt you, then yes, he will be your shadow when I'm not around."

"But I'm not in danger."

He narrows his dark eyes at me. "How do you know?"

"Why would I be?"

"The De Luca crime family has enemies everywhere. We are the highest-ranking mafia family in the world. No one likes a man on top and they will destroy everything you care for before taking your kingdom. You are the only thing besides Brixley that I care for. You're always in danger."

I shiver. A kind, nerdy boy would have been nice right about now, but no, it had to be this broody tatted man I fell for. Or more like, took me. Doesn't matter anymore. "Which brings me to my next problem. You need to learn to shoot."

"I don't really like guns."

"Better make this one your best friend because it will go with you everywhere."

Only one month in as a mafia wife and I'm already exhausted.

BRIXLEY SQUEEZES ME IN A DEATH GRIP AS HER WILD COPPER HAIR gets in my face. "I've missed you so much," she says, pulling back to look at me. "How was the honeymoon?"

"It was… different."

"Different good or different bad?" She raises an eyebrow.

"Both?" It's true. Some parts were amazing while others just hurt.

She looks over my shoulder, eyes narrowed at Adriano. "Who's the meathead?"

"Bodyguard," I sigh, looking over my shoulder at my shadow.

"You don't need a bodyguard when you're with me." She pulls out her phone, hitting a couple of buttons before bringing it to her ear. "Don't appreciate your shadow, Satan. I can take care of us all on my own." She pauses, lips thinning as she listens. "But did I die? No. I survived every attack last year with great ease." I hear a bark of laughter on the other end and my lips curl. "Fine. Let's see how great your security puppy is." She grins, pocketing her phone. "Feel like rebelling, Prim?"

I grin. "Absolutely."

My phone rings and I look down at it. "Ignore it." Brixley tosses her hair over her shoulder. Climbing into her car and honking the horn for me.

I look over my shoulder, sticking my tongue out at Adriano who narrows his eyes at me. I jump in the car and Brix barrels down the road. I grab onto the oh-shit handle as I giggle. Miley Cyrus's "Plastic Hearts" blares from the speakers as Brix takes a sharp turn, causing my head to smack the window, but I continue to laugh. I look in the side mirror and see no sign of Adriano. Brixley's phone rings through the car speakers, pausing the song.

"Hello," she singsongs.

"What are you doing?" Amiyah's cheerful voice comes through, making me smile.

"Prim and I are rebelling," Brixley says with a smirk on her face.

"Without me?" Amiyah mock gasps. "You bitches. Come get me."

"On our way." Brix ends the call, taking a turn onto campus and stopping at The Misfits' house.

Beckett walks out shaking his head as Brixley rolls the

window down. "What kind of trouble are you getting into?" he asks, placing a kiss to her forehead.

"Not much." She smiles sweetly.

"Really? Tell me why I have an angry Vance on my phone. Pretty sure he's cussing at me in Italian."

Brixley rolls her eyes. "He is so dramatic. I'm just taking my friends into town."

"And evading security details," Beckett supplies. You can tell he's worried, but clipping Brixley's wings would result in her leaving him.

"Exactly." Brixley smiles.

Amiyah runs out of the house, a giant smile on her face as she climbs in the back seat. "Are we shopping on Beckett's money?" she teases.

"Not a chance in hell," Beckett replies, kissing Brixley quickly and walking away.

We pull out of campus and Brixley takes a left instead of a right. "Umm, where are we going?"

"Out of town."

I raise my eyebrows. "To where?"

She shrugs her shoulders. "Wherever the car takes us."

Amiyah laughs in the back seat, and then screams, "Girls' trip!"

"Classes start again in three days," I stress.

"We'll be back in time. I'll make sure of it."

"Brixley, I did not sign up for camping. Ew, is that a bug?" Amiyah whines.

We stopped at a store earlier and got all the essential things we needed. Like tents, coolers, and food to put in them. Just whatever Brixley could think of since she is the only one who has ever been camping.

"Oh, hush. It'll be fun," Brixley says, putting up the giant tent we are all going to share.

"Does anyone even know where we are?"

Brixley shakes her head. "No."

"Not to be that person but we all almost died last semester, shouldn't we be more careful than this?"

"Can't live life in fear, Prim. Or you will never truly live," Brixley says.

"Listen to you, sounding like a philosopher no one asked for," Amiyah says, swatting something away from her face.

I sit in the lawn chair, taking in the bright moon and twinkling stars that blanket the sky. Maybe this is what I needed, a moment away from him. Things have moved so fast and it's so confusing it makes me dizzy. He's so protective but highly grumpy. He doesn't follow rules but expects me to. It's in my nature to be a pushover, and I honestly don't find it a flaw as some do, but I think mutual respect would have been nice. Not that I minded when he took me on every surface in the condo. It's too late to establish boundaries now. I let him tear every one of mine down. Now, I just need to do the same with his.

He says he's not sure he can love, but I've seen him love his sister. I think he is capable but sees it as a weakness. I'm sure mafia princes are not supposed to have weaknesses. I don't know much about his world but that just seems like a simple fact. But I want the great love I see in movies and read about in books. Even if the journey is long and hard. Unfittingly, I want that with Vance. Spending close to a month with only him was the damning of my heart. I fall easily due to never having much love in my life. And I think if he'd allow me in, surrender to what we were always meant to be, he could love me like I deserve. I know he's given me his secret, but I still feel like there is a wall between us. Like he doesn't truly let me in. I can't explain it, it's just a feeling.

My phone pings, jerking me out of my sad haze as I look down.

Vance: Are you safe?

Me: Yes.

Vance: I haven't jerked off in a while, but since my wife is gone and I crave her, I have no choice.

A picture comes through, and my mouth drops open. His big, tatted hand is wrapped around his shaft. The head red and angry. I swallow, my core aching with need. My cheeks heat as I look around to make sure the girls aren't paying attention.

Vance: This is beneath me.

Me: It looks like you have it under control.

Vance: I could use some inspiration.

I look around at the campsite, literally nowhere to hide and do this.

Me: Hold on.

I rise, rubbing my sweaty palms on my jean shorts. "I'm going to walk to the bathroom." I point in the direction to it.

Amiyah and Brixley both look up. "Do you want us to come?"

"Oh, no." I shake my head quickly. Too quickly, probably.

"Okay..." Amiyah studies me. "See you soon or else we'll come looking for you."

I force a smile. "Okay."

I walk across the path, turning for the water stream

instead of the bathroom. Driving in, I saw a lot of coverage in the trees. Sliding into the dense trees and bushes, I unbutton my shorts, allowing them to slip down my legs. I sit on the rock, spreading my legs wide and blushing fiercely. I've never done anything like this in my life, but Vance awakens something in me. I position the phone between my legs, pulling up my shirt to expose my hip bones all the way to The Misfits tattoo and showing a hint of his brand. I angle the phone, all of that on display, and then snap it. I have to give it a couple of takes since my hand is shaking so hard. But finally, I take one I'm pleased with and hit Send. My phone rings and Vance's name flashes on the screen. I answer it.

"Baby girl, where are you? I'm coming to get you."

I giggle. "I'm not telling you."

He groans, his breaths choppy. "Keep talking to me, Angel," he grunts.

"Are you... touching yourself?"

"Are you?" he rasps.

"Should I?" I ask shyly.

"Fuck yes. But you better hope no one sees my pussy, Angel." I run my finger through my slick folds, my eyes closing as a tiny moan escapes. "Good girl," he growls. And I melt into the rock. "Push three fingers inside your desperate cunt." I do, listening to his breathing pick up as he works himself.

"Vance," I say breathlessly.

"Fuck," he hisses. "Fuck yourself with your small fingers. Go fast, Primrose. I'm close and we are going to come together." I do as he says, moaning as I fuck myself to his groans and moans. "Pinch your clit. You like that." I do, and it's all I need to come, spasming around my fingers.

Vance moans, and I think he comes with me. "Now," he says breathlessly. "Put your cum-soaked fingers in your mouth."

I do and my phone beeps with a FaceTime request. I answer and Vance appears on the screen, lying in bed. His muscular, tatted chest moves up and down as he bites hard on his bottom lips at the sight of me. "When I get my hands on you, I'm going to fuck you so hard for disappearing on me."

I pull my fingers out, licking them greedily, and he curses. "I should be back soon." I smile.

"Show me the view." I turn the camera view to let him see the stream of water and forest. Turning it back to front-facing, I see him smirking. "No, I'll be seeing you soon. Night, Angel." And then he hangs up.

Shit.

16
VANCE

Beckett and I speed in the direction of the camping grounds. Primrose has no clue how much trouble she's in. Maybe if I showed her the death threats she'd take me seriously, but I want to protect her from that. Either way, she shouldn't fucking test me like this. The only reason I haven't lost my mind is because she's with Brixley. I know she'll take care of her.

"The speed limit is sixty-five, not eighty."

"I'll let you know when I give a fuck, Beck." Fucker always drives like an old lady. Me? I drive like I have a dying wish.

"I'm just trying to make it there in one piece," Beckett says with boredom.

"Should have taken your own car then."

We both grow quiet after that, until he says, "You think Primrose is ready to initiate someone in this year?"

I shrug but squeeze the fuck out of the steering wheel. "It's up to her. It's not a requirement."

"Not sure where we will do it since someone burned the church down."

"Cemetery. Church sucked anyways. I'm glad it's gone."

Beckett sighs. "Yeah, the memories there are tainted. Brixley never wanted to go back, and she used to love it there."

"Soulless ready to initiate some people?"

Beckett laughs. "You know she is. Primrose, Amiyah, Madden, and Brixley are the only ones who need to do it if they choose."

We pull in at the campground, and I immediately spot the black G-Wagon. I park the car, climbing out to see the girls all sitting in a circle, Brixley trying and failing at open-fire cooking. They all look up once Beckett's and my doors shut.

"Oh, no," Primrose whispers.

"Left your security puppy in the dust, Satan." Brixley smiles proudly.

"No, you didn't. I told him to let you go." I'm lying but I can't let this little shit know that. Her head is big enough.

I turn over my shoulder as I hear a car approach. It stops and my heart rate picks up as the window rolls down. I look to Primrose who has a red dot on her head.

"Everyone down," I yell as I tackle Primrose just as the bullet flies past us. I hear Amiyah scream, but I tune her out as I point my gun at the car, shooting as their tires squeal. I look down to Primrose, her eyes are so wide with moister on her lashes. She shakes beneath me, fisting my shirt in her hands. "You're okay," I whisper.

She nods, but her eyes are coated in shock like a foggy view into a window. I lift myself off of her, grabbing her under her knees and picking her up. "I'm taking her home. This, Brixley, is why we don't lose our fucking security detail," I snap, and Brixley flinches away from me.

In all the times I've spoken to my sister, I've never snapped at her, but I need her to understand the gravity of the situation. You think last year would have taught her something, but obviously not.

I carry Primrose to my car, strapping her into the passenger seat and shutting the door. I make my way around and stop as I see Brixley approach me. "I'm sorry, Vance. I just wanted to give her a little break from her new life."

"It's all right, Soulless. Just... listen to me when it comes to my wife. Her world is different than yours now. She's inherited my enemies."

Brixley nods, reaching up on her tippy-toes to kiss my cheek, and sadly, it burns and I would love to push her away. But I hold my ground when it comes to her, like always. "See you at the house."

"We're staying at mine this semester," I respond.

Brixley looks sad but doesn't say anything, so I climb in and take off. "You okay, Angel?"

She doesn't respond as she stares out the window. I need to take her to my parents' house so I can report this to my dad. See if we can narrow down who fucking did this and how long I'm going to torture them.

I LEAVE PRIMROSE DOWNSTAIRS WITH MY MOTHER AS I STORM INTO my father's office. He raises an eyebrow, blowing a smoke ring into the air.

"Son, wasn't expecting you."

I pull my pack out, stuffing my own cigarette in my mouth and lighting it. I close my eyes as the nicotine takes over my mind. "Wasn't planning on coming by," I admit.

"Marriage troubles already?" He chuckles.

"No, but someone tried to shoot her today."

That grabs his attention and he rises from his chair. "Who?"

I blow smoke out of my nose. "I don't know. They never got out of the car and the car was blacked out, no plates."

He rubs his chin. "Where was Adriano?"

"Not there," I say with gritted teeth.

"That fucking nephew of mine. I'm calling my sister to get ahold of her son before I do. This is why he was not chosen as the head. He is not strong enough for this world. I don't care if he is older than you."

"Wait, Adriano was supposed to inherit your title?"

"First male born in the family, but the board and I voted him out. Too weak even as a child."

I nod. "He doesn't seem too bothered by it."

"He's not, but my sister is." My father sighs. "Anyway, tell me more about this attempted assassination."

"We've been getting threats, but I figure it was like the ones you get with Mom. So, I didn't worry about it."

My father narrows his eyes. "Every threat toward your mother fucking dies in a week. It doesn't matter if it's from another gang or the fucking milk man, I eliminate them. Come on, I've raised you better than this."

I grind my molars, looking away. "We don't know who it is."

"Hmm... I see. They usually are very stupid and leave a clue. But no clue?" I shake my head in response. "I see. Let me look into this, son. Until then, you keep a close eye on Primrose and use someone besides Adriano to watch her."

"I don't trust anyone," I say.

"Then you follow her. You need her alive for you to take my role. If she's not, I'll be forced to pick you a new wife, and quickly."

The way he disregards her leaves a sour taste in my mouth. I glare at him, blowing smoke in his face. "Let's get something straight. I don't care who the fuck you are, you don't talk about her like she's replaceable. I'm either with her or no one at all. And you can go fuck your kingdom if you think differently."

As I walk out, I hear him chuckle but I'm too furious to pay any attention to him.

I DROP MY HEAD UNDER ONE OF THE MANY SHOWERHEADS, SIGHING deeply. I was right there and still, I almost lost her. I can protect any other person, but when it comes to her, I fail every fucking time. I need to get her out of my head so I can protect her.

"Vance," she speaks softly. I turn to see her supple body as she walks closer to me in the shower room. Her light hair darkens as the water drips over it. Water like raindrops moving over every curve of her body. If she wasn't so fucking sweet, so beautiful, I wouldn't care as much.

She's the light to my dark. She complements me in every way. It makes it impossible to push her away.

"How are you doing?" I ask.

"I'm fine. I just... Can I wash you?" she asks softly.

I shake my head. "I don't think it's a good idea."

"It's intimate, not sexual."

She has a good point and after the day she's had, I can't find it in me to disappoint her. "Okay, but if I say stop, you stop. If I look like I've zoned out, you run. These are the rules, Primrose. Got it?"

She nods, grabbing my body wash that smells of coffee and whiskey. She pours a generous amount in her hand and steps up to me. "If this works, I get to touch you from now on. Whenever I please."

I don't say anything. I close my eyes as her hands lay on my arms. Taking a deep breath as she moves them over both my shoulders. Her hands meet on my chest, and I relax into the tile wall behind me, my eyes cracking open to watch her expressive doe eyes as she traces every inch of my body she's touching. Her hands roam over my abs, fingers trailing along the grooves. She runs her hands over my abdomen, fingers playing with my happy trail, and my dick grows fucking hard. Hard from her touch. The last time this happened I was screaming in my mind for it to not react, but this time, my soul sings in triumph that I'm not as fucked up as I thought I was.

She moves her hands over my hips, gliding down my thighs. She drops to her knees, using more body wash to massage my calves. "Turn around, please."

I do, my head resting on the wall as she washes my legs, skipping over my ass out of fear like she did my dick, I presume. She works her small hands over my back muscles and I close my eyes, my stiff body looser than it's been in a while. I feel her hands on my shoulders and then I feel her place a soft kiss on my spine.

"You're done," she whispers.

I spin, grabbing her by the neck and slamming her back into the tile wall. "Stop breaking down my walls," I hiss. Mad at her for fixing everything hard about me. Making me soft in a world that has no room for it. "I want you to sleep in your own room. Our honeymoon is over and so are we.

You're my wife. You spread your legs for me when and if I feel like it. But other than that, I have no use for you. Maybe a couple of heirs in a couple of years." I squeeze her neck, fucking hating myself but knowing she'll be my downfall if I don't stop this. "Now, leave." I let go of her throat and she slides down the wall, cupping her neck. She looks at me with unshed tears that gut me.

"Do not come to me tonight, or tomorrow, ever," she says rising.

"If you don't give it to me, I'll have to find a mistress."

She lets out a sad laugh. "Good luck, Vance. You can barely touch yourself."

And then she's gone. But it's better this way. The less important she is to me, the safer her life will be and the harder my heart will be.

17
PRIMROSE

I STARE IN THE MIRROR, embracing my scar, finding the beauty in it for the first time ever. I pull out the white glitter stick Amiyah gave me. She said it's for raves, but it'll give me an edge. I roll it over the scar, giggling as I stare at it. I actually like it. I grab my bag with my sketchbooks. I finished all my basics last year, so this year I will be solely focused on creating my art. I walk down to the kitchen, spotting Adriano. "Will you drive me to school, please?"

He rubs the back of his neck, looking uncomfortable. "Isn't Vance taking you?"

I shake my head. "No, you are because I'm asking you to. If you work for him that means you work for me, right?"

He nods. "Yeah, come on." He sighs. Like this is the last thing he wants to do. I get that I've put him in a tight position, but I refuse to ride with my husband today.

I follow him to the car and climb in, putting my AirPods in to listen to Lana Del Rey. She's my favorite singer in the entire history of music. Her beats, her voice, her words... there is no one who can compare.

I don't know what happened between Vance and me.

Maybe I touched him too soon? Maybe he wasn't ready, but to me, he felt ready. His body was soft under my touch, breaths even as if he was at peace. But the way he slammed me to the wall, squeezed my throat until I couldn't breathe, and God... the words he said to me... It's not something I can just let go of. I haven't spoken to him since. He did stop to tell me he would be driving me to school today, but I ignored him. I knew he wouldn't be up before me, so I snuck out. Thankful Adriano was already here so I didn't have to call Brixley. She'd be so mad that I woke her up this early.

We drive past the gates of the college, and I step out after Adriano parks. Spotting Amiyah, I head to the coffee shop.

"Prim, why do you look so sad?" she asks with a pout.

"No reason, it's just early and I miss living with you and Brix." It's not a lie, I do miss The Misfits' house.

"You know you can come over whenever." She knocks her sunglasses down, eyeing Adriano with interest. "Your shadow is welcomed as well."

I lightly hit her shoulder. "Come on, I need some hot chocolate."

Amiyah sighs. "Don't remind me. I can't believe you drink hot chocolate instead of the nectar of the gods."

I laugh. "It's too bitter."

"Creamers and sugar," she deadpans.

I shake my head. "No, that doesn't really work for me."

We walk into the coffee shop and give our orders. Amiyah eyes Adriano while we wait and I roll my eyes, sending a text to Brixley to see if she's up yet. She usually makes Mondays her off days, whereas I did weekend classes to finish quicker. We are so opposite but it works for us. Honestly, our whole group shouldn't work. Brixley the badass, Amiyah the materialistic girl, and me, the sweet innocent one. But somehow, we all click.

I grab my hot chocolate from the counter and take a window seat with Amiyah. She tells me about the theater arts classes she's taking this year and I listen as I sip, until a hand wraps around my arm and jerks me up.

"*Wife*, we need to talk," Vance hisses.

"Don't grab her like that," Amiyah snaps, standing up.

"It's all right." I jerk my arm from his grip, glaring at him. "I'll see you at lunch, Miya."

I grab my hot chocolate, throwing my bag over my shoulder and walking out of the coffee shop. I stop under a tree, turning to look at Vance.

"What?" My voice is so cold I barely recognize it.

"I told you I would take you to school. So why is it when I wake up, you're already gone?"

I take a deep breath, numbing my heart from this man. "I'm your wife. Only used to spread my legs when you please. That is my job, my only requirement. I don't have to tell you where I'm at as long as I have Adriano."

I cross my arms and Vance cages me into the tree, his thick arms trapping me. "And if I want you to spread your legs now?"

Not the time or place to be feeling aroused, but it doesn't stop my body. It hasn't gotten the memo that this man is an asshole. "I'd tell you to go find a mistress." I shove on his chest, moving away from him.

"Angel."

"Don't call me that," I yell over my shoulder. "I'm a warm hole for you and nothing else. Go fuck yourself, *husband*."

The needle sticks into my finger as a small dab of blood comes to the surface. I bit my lip, wiping the blood on my jacket because I have nowhere else to wipe it. This is what happens when you're distracted.

"Are you okay?" Adriano asks.

"Yeah, just not paying attention." I narrow my eyes at him. "I don't understand why you are even allowed in here." It's true. You don't see anyone else with a bodyguard and the professor looks over him as if he is not there.

Adriano gives me a blank look, and then arches an eyebrow. "Really? You married one of the scariest men in the world and you don't understand why no one questions his actions? You don't mess with the De Lucas, and here on your prestigious, little campus, no one messes with The Misfits. So, you got both of those things going for you."

I'm about to respond, when the professor's voice jerks me to attention. "This project needs to be finished by next week. I want the best ball gown you can create." She's a no rest type of woman. It's day one and I already have an assignment from her. "You are dismissed. Take your project home if you wish, but make sure to bring it back every day. I want to watch everyone's progress."

I open my bag, stuffing my sketchbook and scraps of fabric in there. I stand and my head swims. Tiny black dots covering my vision.

"Whoa," Adriano says, helping me sit back down.

"It's fine, I just stood up too quickly." I rise again, but Adriano keeps his hand on my elbow as he leads me to the car. He opens the door and I climb in. "I promise, I'm fine," I say to him.

He nods. "If you say so."

We drive the rest of the way in silence. My classes took longer today than I had anticipated, which means my husband is waiting for me in the dining room when Adriano drops me off.

"Come eat," he says.

"No, thank you."

"Wasn't a request. Sit."

I spin to face him. He knows how my father was and now he's treating me just like him. "You know what?" I flip my dinner onto the floor like a child. The plate shattering, food scattering and rolling across the floor. "Fuck you. I don't know what your problem is, but I'm over it."

Vance rises slowly, sitting his glass down next to an almost empty bottle of whiskey. As he approaches me, I can smell it, wafting from his pores so strong you'd think he bathed in it. He tugs on the front strands of my hair, his hand moving to the back of my head and twisting sharply as he smashes our lips together. I moan, lost for a second, but then I push on his chest.

"Stop it."

He grins as I take a step back. "That's not what you really want, is it, *wife*?"

He pulls his bandana out from his pocket, looking down at it. "Let's play a game. You run and if I catch you, I get to have you."

"Vance," I try to speak, but he begins counting.

"One."

A thrill shoots up me as I take a step back, and then another.

Do I want to be hunted down?

"Two."

He didn't tell me how long he would count so I don't have time to ponder the question as I take off. Running for the front door and throwing it open. Not caring that it's not shut. There is nothing but forest out here and it'll be so easy to get lost in there, but my adrenaline takes over me. I duck to the right of the house, hoping he thinks I'm crazy enough to run into the forest. I take the steps up to the back porch, avoiding the pool and hot tub. Thinking I can sneak back inside and lock my door. A hand fists my hair, pulling back so hard my neck stretches. I crash to the porch, my dress rising as a hard body lands on top of me from behind.

"Got you," he rasps.

I peek over to see his dark eyes glow above the bandana, and something unlocks inside me. Something dark and twisted, because I want him to take me like this. He pushes my head into the stone of the porch, ripping my dress from behind me to leave me exposed in my panties. The cool night of Washington makes my body break out in goosebumps and I shiver. Vance's hands roughly grab my ass, his fingernails sinking into the flesh before his teeth follow suit. The pain is sharp but leaves a gooey mess between my thighs. I hear his zipper and then he is thrusting into me with one long punishing thrust. He doesn't bind me this time, but I guess he doesn't need to since his heavy weight is keeping me pinned down as he wrecks me from behind.

It feels like a punishment as he rasps, "You're being a dirty slut today. Throwing your food like a child, running from me, telling me to fuck off. Not once, but twice. That's not how my angel acts."

I cry out when his teeth sink into my shoulder. His hand comes around, forcing my mouth open as he pushes his fingers down my throat, choking me until I have saliva covering my lips.

I cough as he pulls out of me, but then I feel him at my back entrance. He slaps my ass, hard, and then slowly enters with his tip. I tense up.

"Relax, it will only hurt if you fight me."

Vance's hand comes under me, lifting me to my knees as his fingers play roughly with my pussy, making my body sing for him as he enters me even more until finally, he's all the way in.

I feel so full with his thick length in my ass and his fingers slowly fucking me. "Your pussy is a slut too, all messy with my cock in your ass." He scrapes his teeth along my back, slapping my pussy roughly. "I knew you'd be perfect, I just never dreamed you'd be made to be my perfect fuck doll." He thrusts. "Isn't that right, baby girl? You're nothing but a warm hole for me to use up until I ruin it for other men." He thrusts harder this time and I moan. "Toss you away when I've had my fill and move on to my mistress."

I reach behind me, my nails sinking and scraping down his thighs, hoping to draw blood.

"You trying to mark me, Angel?" I don't respond and he leans closer to my ear and hisses, "Too fucking late. You already have." He jerks me back by my hair, smashing our bodies together. One hand plays with my heat while the other wraps around my throat. Not squeezing but it feels like a collar, and I think I love that too.

He works my body until I'm screaming his name. Both of us drenched in sweat as he continuously marks me. He removes his hand so he can leave bruising hickeys and bite marks along my neck, across my shoulder, anywhere his lips can meet my skin. Then, finally we come. Together. He jerks out and comes on my ass.

I fall forward onto my stomach. My eyes closing with exhaustion and the need to sleep. I feel him lift me in his arms as I rest my head on his shoulder. My mind is drifting now that I'm safely in his arms.

I WAKE WITH A STRONG BODY HOLDING MINE TIGHTLY. I MOAN AND not with pleasure... My head throbs and when I let out a rough cough, my throat burns with an intensity that makes me want to cry. It feels so raw and sore I don't want to speak.

"Are you okay?" Vance mumbles into my back, his hand finding my forehead as he presses down. "You're burning up."

"I don't know how," I say, body shivering and teeth chattering.

Vance moves, flipping on the lamp next to the bed and basking the room in a soft glow. He peers over me, brow furrowed.

"I'm calling the doctor."

"I'm sure I'm fine, just a small cold," I manage to get out, only to be thrown into a coughing fit.

"Small colds don't come with high fevers." He grabs his phone from the nightstand and starts to make a call. I follow him under the covers. Curling into his body for the heat and comfort.

The doctor gets here a little while later. He checks my temperature and winces. And then asks me about my symptoms. "It sounds like strep throat, but I'll need to run a test." He takes out a long cotton swab and I grimace. "I won't lie, this will hurt but it'll be over soon."

He swipes my throat and tears sting my eyes as he walks over to his bag and pulls out a tube. I lay back down, wishing I had my mom. She was always so amazing when I was sick. Taking care of me and letting me watch cartoons. I long to feel her lips on my temple as a way to see if my fever was any better.

The doctor does a rapid strep test and ten minutes later, I test positive. "I'm going to prescribe you some antibiotics. Your husband can pick them up in the morning. For now, take some Tylenol and try to get some rest. You can eat some honey, gargle warm salt water. And make sure to drink plenty of water. I'm also leaving you some suckers that will numb your throat." He pats my leg beneath the covers. "Get to feeling better, Primrose."

"Thank you," I croak, my eyes shutting as the doctor and Vance leave the room. I must have dozed off because when I wake up, Vance has his hand pressed to my head again. A white pharmacy bag sits on the nightstand beside me along with a glass of water.

"How are you feeling?" he asks gently, but I knock his hand away.

I haven't forgotten that we technically are not getting along, or how he's been acting toward me. I grab my medicine and water and walk across to my room. Shutting the door. It doesn't take him long to follow, his arms crossed over his expansive chest as he leans against the door.

"I know you're mad, but I can take care of you."

"Not in our arrangement. Call Adriano. He can take care of me."

He stalks to me after I swallow my medicine. Lifting me by my waist, he throws me over his shoulder. "I'm not calling fucking Adriano." He walks across the hallway, back to his room. "Stop being stubborn and let me help you."

"I just want to sleep." My voice trembles.

He lays me down gently on the bed. "After you eat, you can, but I'm the one taking care of you. So, get that through your pretty little head." He tosses the remote at me and leaves the room.

I don't really watch TV. I have no clue what to even put on, so I pull up Netflix and settle on a murder documentary. It may seem out of character for me, but I find it oddly fascinating. I also like to try and guess who it is before they reveal it. I snuggle into the fluffy bed, getting comfortable as the narrator begins. I think the original *Forensic Files* narration is hands down the best. No one's voice is as chilling or entertaining as his. You get a lot that are monotonous, as if their sole purpose is to put people to sleep. Just like this one.

Vance reemerges, placing a serving tray over my lap with what looks like oatmeal. There is also a steaming cup of tea. "Honey and vanilla chamomile tea with lemon. It's supposed to help with your sore throat, but who the hell knows." He takes his jeans off, giving me a view of his tight briefs before he slides some sweats on. He yanks his shirt off, tossing it to the floor. "Do you want me to get you some clothes or are you okay in my t-shirt from last night?"

"Your t-shirt is fine." I begin to eat, drinking my tea. Surprisingly, I start to feel a little better, but my eyes grow heavy as he removes the tray and comes to lay back beside me. He tucks an arm under my head, his body close to mine as his hand lays on my forehead. He kisses the side of my face, mumbling something I don't quite pick up as I fall asleep in his bed.

Just until I feel better.

18

VANCE

I PLACE my phone and wallet in my slacks, unbuttoning a few of the top buttons on my black dress shirt. It's Saturday and Primrose is finally starting to feel a little better. She's spent a week in bed, watching murder documentaries and working on her dress while I begrudgingly went to class. Tonight, we have a charity gala. Not a Misfits one but a De Luca one. The place will be crawling with criminals of all kinds. It's not somewhere I want to take my angel, but this is her world now.

Primrose walks in, her long blonde hair over her face as she attempts to hide her scar. A simple silk red dress wraps around her breasts, thin straps the only thing keeping them from spilling out. It hugs her waist like a second skin over her wide hips. It's classic and simple, everything I would expect from her.

Except, the jacket is odd. "Why do you have a jacket on?"

She looks up, eyes wide and so blue they look like pools of frozen water. Her lashes are full and black. The minimal makeup gives her an innocent look that most women in an outfit like this cannot pull off.

"You left marks all over my neck and chest."

I smirk, last night she kept pushing her ass into my dick and I finally had enough. Sick or not, I had to have her. So, I took her. I walk around her, pausing at her back as I pull her jacket off. I brush her hair behind her shoulder and bend down by her ear. "Embrace your scars, Angel," I whisper.

She nods. "Just because I allow you to have me," I chuckle, and she glares, "doesn't mean you get to *have me*. I haven't forgotten the words you said, how you treated me, when you got scared."

"I'm not scared of anything," I grind out.

She turns, her hand resting on my cheek, thumb trailing over my faint scar. "Holding on to your trauma doesn't make you strong, surviving them does. We don't have to let them define us. You can still be strong and let go of that sad, angry little boy."

"Hands off," I snap.

She smiles sadly, letting her hand drop. "Maybe in time you'll see. But by then, it'll be too late to fix this."

She walks away and I sigh, pulling my hair between my fingers.

Prim doesn't see it now, but someday she will. I push her away to protect her. I won't let her go, but I refuse to be the reason she is hurt again.

PRIMROSE

My face physically hurts from smiling. I've met so many people and yet, I still can't tell you who is who. Everyone keeps looking at my scar and then quickly looking away as they shake my hand. I make them uncomfortable. I can tell by how they can't hold eye contact very long and always end up talking to Vance to avoid me. It stings. Makes me want to hide, but I promised myself I wouldn't do that, not anymore.

I think the worst part is when the women see me and immediately don't see me as a threat, so they flirt with my husband right in front of me. He never engages them in conversation but the simple fact that they think they can really irritates me.

I squeeze Vance's bicep, not caring he's in the middle of a conversation. He leans down to give me his ear, pausing the gentlemen in front of him. "What is it, Angel?"

"I'm going to get a drink."

"I'll come with you," he says.

"No, finish your conversation, it'll only take me a few minutes." I place a kiss to his cheek. Loving how he doesn't flinch away from me. Hating that it's all part of the happy couple act.

I walk to the bar, asking for a water. I don't really drink, and if I do it's with people I trust. The people in here are vile, I don't care if this is a charity for a scholarship. I bet every man in here partakes in some sort of illegal business, or worse. So, water it is. A lady slides in beside me as I wait for my water.

"He looks happy." I turn my head, my lips thinning as I take in Lucia. She has long black hair and dark tan skin. Her eyes are a vivid caramel and she's picture-book perfect.

"He is," I concur, not really wanting to chat with her but my eyes are watching her every move.

"Shame he was stuck with someone like you. I'm sure you were once pretty, but that scar takes it all away."

I grind my teeth. "Flattery will get you nowhere." She

laughs but abruptly stops when I lean in closer. "Come anywhere near my husband and I'll kill you." Ice drips from my voice and her eyes narrow.

"I'm his aunt."

"Sick way of showing it," I spit.

She pauses, tilting her head. "He told you." I stay quiet as she studies me. "He wanted it. I did him a favor."

So many things I want to say, but I can't say them without yelling. So instead, I put the heel of my stilettos into her toeless ones and press down. She groans softly in pain.

"Like I said," I whisper. "Stay away from my husband or I'll kill you." I smile sweetly, moving back and grabbing my water. "I hope your evening is dreadful." I walk away, coming to stand beside my husband.

He raises an eyebrow to ask silently if I'm okay. I nod, sipping my water as he continues to talk.

"Russian bastards," one man spits and throws back his drink. "They've been trying to take us out for a decade. It's time we handle them properly."

Vance nods. "War is like a game of chess. We have to move smartly. Predict their moves before they make them."

"Or we can just blow up their base outside of town. I hear that is where they keep all their guns and product. It would be a below-the-belt kick that will send a message."

Vance goes to speak but my body is launched backward as fire explodes along the side of the entrance. I hit the floor, gasping as I choke on thick smoke, and my ears ring. I can see the commotion around me but all I can hear is a constant ringing.

I push up to my feet, my balance off as I stumble a little. I see people running, others shooting guns at the entrance. I look around and see Vance's mom. I go to her, and her arms wrap around my shoulders as she takes me toward a side exit. I can see her mouth moving but no words form in my mind. I tap my ears and she nods, ducking us out a side entrance and moving us into a car waiting in the alley. We climb in and the car takes off, but Vance and his father are nowhere in sight.

"Where is Vance?" I ask, the ringing finally dying down a little bit.

Aurora is disheveled. Her hair a mess, black soot on her forehead. "They're meeting us at our house once everything is taken care of." She reaches a hand out, turning my chin and checking me over. "You have a cut on your forehead, but I don't think it will scar." She sits back, looking down at her phone.

"Is this normal?" I ask.

She shakes her head. "We haven't been directly attacked in over a decade. Someone new must have entered the playing fields."

I stare out the window. I'm not sure how to feel about my new life. When we were on our honeymoon, nothing like this ever entered my mind. But now that we are back in the real world, outside forces just keep pushing us further apart.

"No, I want you to keep following them. Ram them into a fucking ditch. I don't fucking care. I want to know who they are and why they're targeting us," Vance's father says walking in. He ends the call, grabbing his wife and checking her from head to toe before kissing her forehead. "Are you hurt?" he asks, softly.

She shakes her head. "No, but our daughter is." She points to me.

Mr. De Luca comes over, dropping to his haunches in front of me. "It doesn't look like you'll need stitches. Does your head hurt?" He presses the cut softly and I shake my head. "Good. Why don't you let my wife take you upstairs and get you cleaned up."

"Okay," I whisper, but all I really want to do is wait for my husband. I still don't know if he's okay. I know I should ask, but I'm not comfortable with his family yet. So I follow his mother upstairs.

THE BATHROOM IS LAVISH, BUT NOT AS BIG AS VANCE'S. I ALSO SEE that they don't share the same love for gothic vibes as Vance does. I let the water run over my body until the red and black washes away and the water goes clear. I scrub my body, rinsing my hair twice to make sure the smell of smoke doesn't linger. Once I'm done, I rest my body against the tile, allowing the steam to surround me.

My eyes shoot open as the shower door swings open. Vance steps in, eyes murderous as he slams the door behind him. The water drenches his hair, causing it to hang over his eyes as his clothes grow heavy. He crowds me into the shower wall, forehead resting against mine as he breathes deeply.

"You're okay?" he asks.

I nod in response. "I'm fine."

He kisses my lips, mumbling, "I'm going to find out who did this."

My hands run over his chest through his clothes, and he

shivers under my touch. His heart pounds beneath my palms and I capture his lips with mine. Sucking on his bottom lip sweetly. I skate my hands up and around his neck. His big palm grabs my thigh, hoisting it over his hip as he presses into me. I continue to be soft with him, kissing him slow and gentle as I moan sweetly into his mouth. He pulls back. "Not at my parents' house." I nod, about to release him, but his hands grab mine and hold them in place.

"Keep touching me a little longer, Angel."

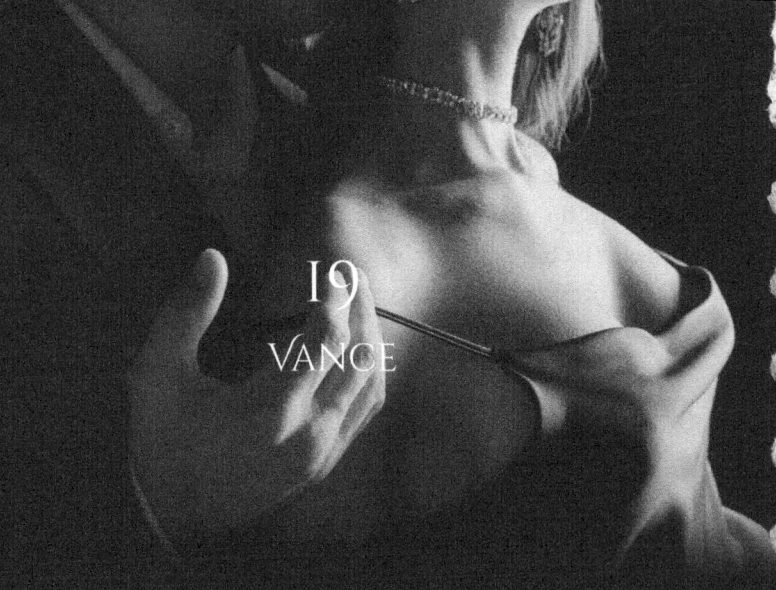

19
VANCE

College was just a way for me to get officially initiated into The Misfits. I never needed it, but then she came, and I wanted to finish. I'm almost done with my bachelor's in business, which isn't going to hurt, but it's not going to help me in life either. I would much rather be at school, stalking my wife from class to class, but instead, I'm smoking a cigarette waiting for this fucker who shot up the gala to wake up.

Adriano plays on his phone in the corner, watching fucking TikTok videos. I see why he was voted out; he could never make it. I left Madden in charge of Primrose. Not that Beckett couldn't, but Primrose seems to like Madden a little more. It's the calm presence he gives off. I get it—don't like it, but I get it.

Adriano looks up and then down at the man who's tied by his hands and feet into a modern-day torture tub. "Why a tub?" he asks.

"Have you ever read about medieval torture devices?" I ask, blowing a thick cloud of smoke out. He shakes his head. "They're highly fascinating. As long as you don't find yourself falling victim to them."

The man stirs and starts jerking his hands and feet. "What the fuck?" he hisses.

"What the fuck is right." I walk over to him, kicking the tub and making the man curse. "Who the fuck sent you to blow up our gala?"

The man laughs. "You think tying me to some tub is going to get me to talk? *Fica ignorante*." He spits. *Ignorant cunt.*

I grin. "No, but I was kind of hoping you wouldn't take the easy way out and I'd get to test this method out. You're my first, this is a very special moment for us." I pull a bucket of honey over and dump it on his head, so it covers his body.

"*Bastardo*," he curses. *Bastard.* "What is this?" he asks, trying to move the honey from his eyes.

"Honey."

"Honey?" Adriano asks. I cast him a look and he looks away, hands in his pockets.

"I'm going to give you one more chance to tell me who sent you."

"Give me your worst, *bastardo*."

I shrug, opening the white wooden box to release the bees, and then I hit Record on the camera. "Out, Adriano. What comes out of this next box is not to be messed around with." Adriano moves quickly as the man screams inside the wooden tub. I can see his face already swelling up. I press the timer on the next white box and quickly exit, locking the door.

Pulling up my phone, Adriano and I watch as tsetse flies fly out. "What are those?" Adriano asks.

"Tsetse flies, they cause the sleeping sickness."

"Where the fuck do you find those?" he asks, getting a closer look as the man wails. He probably won't make it to feel the effects of the flies, but I like the idea of it.

"Everything is in reach when you have the right connections."

"Do you think he will confess?"

"If he was going to confess, he would have done so the moment he woke up. Besides, this is more of a present. Once he's dead, I'll drop him off to where someone from the media will capture the story. They'll know we're coming for them. It's only a matter of time."

I click the phone off and walk to my car. The fact that my dad can't figure out who's doing this puts me on edge, but I did learn something today. Whoever it is, they're Italian. Which means they're close. Too fucking close.

"Honey," Primrose calls, and I glare as she walks into the kitchen. Her pet name for me is the furthest thing I could ever be, but she refuses to stop calling me that. "I brought your sister home with me."

"What about her fuckhead boyfriend?"

"Present." Beckett steps around, flipping me the finger.

Brixley walks in behind him, kissing my cheek. I grit my teeth to suppress the flinch. "Satan."

"Did you bring my fucking cat back yet?"

She shakes her head. "Primrose and I have joint custody."

"How about I buy you your own cat and you bring Samson home?"

"No dice." She smiles, pinching my cheek. *Brat.*

Madden and Amiyah walk in next, neither of them looking or speaking to one another. Not my story to tell but they are only fooling themselves. "Time to pick some new recruits," Amiyah claps, placing her purse on the table.

Primrose tries to walk past me, but I grab her hand, pulling her into my lap and nuzzling my face into the back of her neck. I never thought I would crave someone's touch, their affection, but I'm highly addicted to my wife's. "I want you to sit this year out until I can figure out who's after my family."

She turns her head, looking down at me. "I don't want to hurt people anyway. Remember when you drugged me and stuck me in a cave? My challenge was by far the hardest. My arms have never hurt so bad."

I chuckle, kissing her neck. "Had to prove your worth. You got off easy the entire time. I was always there to protect you." She nods at that. "Besides, at least you didn't eat glass like Amiyah's victim or eggshells like Brixley."

"I am thankful for the marshmallow," she muses.

I turn to face everyone. "Out of my house."

Amiyah pouts. "You're not letting her do it, are you?"

"I don't want to," Primrose states. Her hand twisting in mine in her lap.

The girls bitch as they gather their things, flipping me off as they leave. Primrose leans close to my face. "Want to make love?" she asks.

"I've been torturing someone all day and you ask if I want to make love? No, but I'll fuck you until you're hoarse from screaming my name."

She pushes her lip out in that adorable way that means I'm about to give in. "I want to be in charge."

"You want to ride on top?"

She makes a face. "I want to be in charge completely. My rules."

I lick my lips, wondering how I can deny her. The one thing I'm not into, is losing control of the situation. "Fine."

Her rose petal lips break out into a smile, and I roll my eyes, patting her leg. "Up. Let's get to it."

I follow her upstairs to our room, and she stops at the foot of the bed. "Clothes off, husband. Lay down with your hands above your head."

I chuckle, stripping out of my shirt as her eyes eat me alive. "Is this a little payback?"

She blinks up at me innocently as I unbuckle my pants. "Of course not."

I strip, climbing on the bed and resting my hands above my head. She reaches behind me, pulling up the chain I keep there and cuffs my hands to it. I smirk, pulling against them so she can see I can't get out. This is a huge step for me. Being touched is one thing but being restrained is a whole other level of trust I never thought I would condone to. She climbs off the bed, pulling her dress off to reveal a lacy see-through bodysuit.

"Fuck," I hiss.

She grabs her Misfits bandana and lays it on the bed as she climbs on, crawling to me. She smiles, her tongue coming out to lick my thigh, and my dick stiffens. She moves over my body, her hot core running over me as she bends, laying gentle kisses on my stomach, working her way up my chest until she gently sucks on my neck. I close my eyes, hands pulling fiercely to try to break the cuffs. She nibbles up my chin, stopping a breath away from my mouth as I lean forward to capture hers, but she moves away, sliding her tongue down my torso instead.

"When I get out of these restraints, you're fucked, baby girl."

She ignores me, as if I'm only here for her pleasure and nothing more. Her lips glide around my dick, teasing me with her breath but never touching it. I grunt, thrusting my hips toward her. She's fucking torturing me. She laughs, it's throaty and dripping in honey-sweet lust. Finally, her lips fall on my head as she runs her tongue over the bottom side of my shaft. Her hands run over my ab muscles as she takes me fully in her mouth. I curse low, my head falling back to the pillow. She sucks on my head, her hands working my shaft as she twists her tongue around me. "Fuck, baby girl. I don't know if I should be happy or pissed you can suck my dick so good."

She moans around me, and my balls tighten. My stamina apparently out the window when her mouth is on me. Her fingers run over my balls as she chokes on my dick. She lifts her head, her eyes twinkling as she climbs on top of me, and from this view I can see that her lingerie is crotchless. She wipes her drool from the corner of her mouth before she sinks down, crying out. Her back arches, bringing her breasts close to my face, but I can't fucking reach them. I want to mark her skin so bad for what she's doing to me. "I'm going to punish your ass for this, Angel. My handprints will be a permanent mark on your milky ass as soon as I get my hands on you."

She ignores me again, riding me with long, punishing moves of her hips. I jerk my hips up into her hard, hitting deep inside her. She moans louder, and I fucking come. With no warning. She looks down, cheeks flushed, lips bee-stung from sucking my dick, hair wild.

"Come here and let me out," I say hoarsely.

She lifts up, running her finger through the cum leaking

down her legs, then sucks the digit into her mouth. She climbs off of me and tosses the lingerie, opting for some leggings and a t-shirt. She stuffs her bandana in her waistband, coming to bend over me.

"I'll see you later, honey."

I pull on my restraints, growling, "Where the fuck are you going?"

"To do my duty as a Misfit."

And then she's gone, leaving me strapped to the bed.

20
PRIMROSE

"Do we want to know how you got here without your shadows?" Madden asks, tying his bandana behind his blond hair, brown eyes flashing at Amiyah.

I shake my head, "Probably not, but I want to do this. It's my contribution to our group. I want to give someone the world at their fingertips like I'll get when I graduate."

Madden nods. "Yeah, hopefully they can make it through the trials."

"I don't even know what I'm going to do for mine." I sigh, tying my own bandana.

"Don't worry," Madden says gently, "it'll come to you." He pats my shoulder as he walks over to Brixley. "You sure you can do this?" he asks her.

"Yeah, I don't think we are at risk of another killer this year."

The four of us file into Brixley's G-Wagon; the others can't come since their initiates made it through last year's trials. We drive around campus until we pull up by the dorms. I climb out, a second bandana in my hand as I quickly run to the boys' dorm. There is a boy who was in my class last year, you can tell he's on a scholarship. I see him work two jobs when he's not in class. My heart aches for him a bit, so he's my choice. I sneak into the boys' dorm, going to the second floor and locating Room 249. I jimmy the lock like Madden taught me and the door clicks open. I sit the bandana on Nick's bed and sneak back out. I'm the last back to the car and once I'm in, we drive to The Misfits' house.

"Shit," Brixley whispers.

Vance stands with his arms crossed over his arms, leaning against the hood. We all step out and he rises. "Everyone, go inside." His voice leaves no room for argument, so I follow closely behind Brix. A hand wraps around the back of my neck. "Not you," Vance whispers.

He pulls me to his car, pushing me over the hood so I'm flat on my stomach. "Don't move and don't make a sound," he says sharply, pulling my leggings down harshly. His hand smacks against my ass and I jump, biting into my lip to keep the moan from spilling out. It comes again, sharper this time, his nails digging into my skin, and I do release a small gasp this time. He chuckles roughly, his teeth sinking into my neck as his fingers plunge into me. "Dirty fucking slut," he rasps, and my eyes roll back as he begins rapidly spanking me with his other hand.

The hits come hard and fast, no soothing circles or breaks in between. Just me a crying mess on the hood of his car.

I hear his pants unzip and then I feel him running his hard length between my ass. His hand tangles in my hair as he forces my head back from the cold metal of the car. And then he fucks me. Coming so deep inside me, I leak down both our thighs. His fingers gathering our cum and thrusting it back into me.

"I'm not even close to being done with you," he growls.

I lay in bed, spent, on Vance's chest, as he runs his fingers through my hair. He sighs, rising and stretching his arms.

"Where are you going?" I pout.

"I've got to pack."

I rise, pulling the cover over my chest. "Why?"

"There is something I have to go handle." He reaches for his drawer, slipping on some gray sweatpants.

"How long will you be gone?"

He smiles at me over his shoulder. "Always so curious." He frowns. "I don't know. A month or two. Give or take." He shrugs. "It could be less, but I doubt it."

I bite on my bottom lip. "What do you have to do?"

"Trust me, Angel. It'll be better if you don't know." He walks over to me, kissing my forehead. My hands wrap around his neck, pulling him on top of me. "Just lay with me tonight, you can pack tomorrow."

He runs his finger over my scar lovingly. "Are you going to miss me?"

I smile. "You wish," I whisper brokenly.

21
PRIMROSE

A month and a half later

I wipe the back of my mouth, my other hand reaching up to flush the toilet. I take a deep breath, standing to my feet. Walking over to the sink, I splash water on my face. I look pale, deep circles under my eyes. Brixley and I have caught something, we've both been throwing up for the past week. I'm so nauseous I want to stay in bed all day. But like Brixley, I'm trying to make something of myself, so we don't skip class.

My phone rings and I look down to see a FaceTime request from Vance. I sit the phone against the mirror and swipe to answer.

He takes a drag of his cigarette, blowing smoke at the camera. "You look sick again, Angel. Convince me not to send a fucking doctor to check on you."

I laugh. "I'm fine. When are you coming back?" It's something I ask every morning when he calls.

"I just have a few things to tie up here and then I'm on the first flight back."

I grin. "Good."

He smirks. "Miss me?"

"No, just tired of driving myself to school," I lie.

He laughs. "What do you have planned for today?"

"Amiyah has a play today. So, we're all going to watch that, and then I'm going to have them come stay the night with me. I don't like being alone all the way out here."

He nods. "I get it, but you're not alone. There are twenty men always walking around the house."

I shrug. "Not the same, they won't talk to me."

"I pay them good money to keep their eyes and words away from you."

I roll my eyes. "You're incorrigible."

He smiles at that. "All right, baby girl, I've got to go, but I'll see you soon."

I smile sadly as the call ends and then I throw up. Again.

AMIYAH GLIDES ACROSS THE STAGE IN A VINTAGE-LOOKING WOVEN dress covered in floral print and a white bonnet, her voice thick in a country accent as she wraps her hands around the cowboy dramatically. I'm not going to lie, I'm very much into this. It's a tragic cowboy romance. Right up my alley. Amiyah and the cowboy kiss, and I see Madden stiffen beside me. *Huh, wonder what that's about?*

I throw popcorn in my mouth as I watch Amiyah perform. I laugh with the crowd, swooning anytime he takes his hat off and calls her darling. The show ends and I have tears rolling down my face as Amiyah holds her dead lover in her arms. I didn't get the memo that there was no happily ever after. Madden holds a tissue out for me, and I snatch it, rising to my feet as I clap, whistling for my friend as she and the rest of the cast take a bow.

"I loved it, but it was so sad." I look over to Madden.

He frowns down at me. "Are you okay?"

I shake my head. "If you are not moved by art, just say that, Madden. Don't try to make me feel silly for loving it."

He raises an eyebrow at me as if I'm crazy. I ignore him, wiping my face with the tissue and blowing my nose. Brixley turns to me, eyes narrowed. "Did you seriously cry over that? It's just a play, Prim."

I throw my hands up. "I can't help that I found it to be soul-moving."

"Right... so, your house tonight?"

I nod. "Yeah, just bring everyone."

"Really? You want to have a giant Misfits sleepover?"

"Of course. You guys are my family."

"We are going to go grab our stuff and then we will be there."

I nod, walking toward Adriano. "Sounds good. I'll see you soon."

Adriano furrows his brow at me. "You good?"

I roll my eyes. "Yeah, just really got into the play."

"Gotcha." He nods, leading me to the car.

BRIXLEY AND I LAY ON THE BED AS AMIYAH PEERS DOWN AT US, eyebrows raised. "If I didn't know any better, I would think you're both pregnant."

Brixley shoots up into a sitting position. "Fuck."

"Oh, fuck," Amiyah whispers as Brixley digs her phone out of her pocket.

"Oh shit," Brixley cries as she looks through her calendar. "I'm fucking late."

I rise up too, my eyes wide.

Amiyah sighs. "It was a joke, leave it to you to be actually pregnant. How late are you?"

"Two weeks."

"Lord," Amiyah says, swinging her eyes to me. "Are you late?"

I shake my head. "No. just sick with a stomach flu."

"We have to go get a test. Now." Brixley practically runs for the door, Amiyah and I following after her.

We pull up into town thirty minutes later, swinging by the drug store. Amiyah goes in and purchases a pregnancy test. Once she's back in the car, she tosses the box to Brixley, who says, "I'm not waiting thirty more minutes."

"I'm sure we can find you—" I begin, but stop when Brixley pulls open the front and back doors and squats. "Oh, okay," I mumble.

Brixley pulls up her pants and climbs back into the seat, sitting the test down on the console. She grabs Amiyah's and my hands and sighs. "I don't need a baby right now."

"But babies are so cute," Amiyah says.

"Yeah, plus, I can make you all exclusive baby clothes," I add, trying to lighten the mood.

"That's great and all, but I don't need or want a baby right now. My life is just starting to make sense and I'm finally not screaming in my sleep."

We all stare at the test. "How long does it take?" I ask.

"I bought the best one. A minute, tops."

"This is a long fucking minute," Brixley snaps, closing her eyes.

"Oh, one line so far," Amiyah cheers.

"Miya," I whisper, and she widens her eyes at me.

"I can't look. Are there two lines?" Brixley asks.

I pick up the stick, shining it in the light to see. "No, just one."

"Oh, thank God." Brixley throws the car door open.

"Where are you going?" I ask.

"To buy condoms. I don't trust the birth control I'm using anymore."

Amiyah and I laugh as Brixley runs into the drug store and returns with three bags.

"Damn, girl. How many do you need?" Amiyah questions.

"This may last me a month."

WE ALL LAY IN MY GIANT BED, SNACKS COVERING EVERY AVAILABLE inch as we watch a murder documentary. "It's the uncle," Amiyah says, puffing on a joint.

I wrinkle my nose. "You think? I'm leaning toward the neighbor. He's creepy and has basically stalked her. And he just so happened to be gone the one day she disappears?" I shake my head. "Not buying it."

"It's always the abusive boyfriend," Brixley suggests, petting Samson who smacks his paws at her. "Little shit," she says, tossing my baby at me.

Samson sways his tail, nose up as he prowls toward me. He lays his soft head in my lap, nibbling on my fingers as I pet him. They say cats bite as a form of love, but I wish he'd pick something different to biting because his teeth are so sharp.

"The police questioned the uncle," the narrator says.

"Knew it," Amiyah says, shaking her head.

Brixley laughs, rolling over to face me. "How's married life, Prim?"

Before I got married, I would have told her everything, but since Vance is her brother, it feels wrong.

I plaster on a smile. "It's fine."

"Just because Vance is my brother doesn't mean you can't talk to me, Prim. You'll always be one of my very best friends. Now, tell me the truth."

Amiyah crawls over to lay in front of us, putting her joint out in Vance's favorite empty whiskey glass. Which makes me smile. She's always irritating the guys any way she can.

"It's..." How do I even put into words how he makes me feel? "I..." I sigh. "It's been up and down. I think our honeymoon was the easiest part of this entire relationship. He's so... hot and cold. Like one minute, I'm everything to him, and then the next, I'm his plaything and that's all I'll ever be."

"If I may," Amiyah says, "and trust me, I'm not making any excuses. I'm Team Prim. Ride or die. I'll set Vance on fire for you, but I've known Vance for a very long time and to me, I think you are the one thing in this life that scares the fuck out of him. I've never seen him take an interest in anything other than cars but as soon as he saw you, something in him shifted. Like maybe he could fuck you out of his system and when you didn't give him the chance, he married you. I'll admit, that's some crazy shit, but that's Vance." She shrugs. "I think you took him by surprise. He wasn't expecting you."

Brixley nods. "My brother has a natural-born instinct to protect, and when he can't, it fucking kills him. And he couldn't protect us last semester. I think it made him colder than he was. He probably thinks if he holds you at arm's length, he can protect you better. But don't let him. You deserve to be loved and cherished, Primrose. And if he can't do that, you leave him."

My eyes well and I swallow thickly. My heart warms and breaks all at once. The two emotions of love and war swirling in my stomach. "You just keep breaking his hard exterior with your gentle nature. But don't lay over, give it as good as you get. He doesn't get to treat you like shit because he's scared," Amiyah says, biting into a Twinkie aggressively.

"I love you guys," I sniff.

"Oh, no sappy shit," Brixley says, pretending to throw up. "Now, let's see who the killer is."

"It's the uncle," Amiyah says.

Brixley rolls her eyes. "We'll see, Detective *That Purse Is So Last Year*."

I laugh at them. I may have lost my mom, my only true family, but because of her, I found a new family. One that loves me unconditionally.

And maybe... life won't be so bad.

22
PRIMROSE

My phone buzzes as I sew the seams of the jeans I'm making in my creative fashion design class. I frown, pausing the machine and looking at my phone. I pull up a text from Vance. The message thread is empty because I deleted all my texts last night to free up some storage—no way I was deleting any of the hundreds of pictures of my cat, I need all of them.

Vance: I need you to meet me at your dad's.

I furrow my brow, biting my lip. I haven't spoken to my father since the day of my wedding when he told me not to fuck this up for him. And Vance, he hates him. Why would he even be there?

Me: What, why?
Vance: It's an emergency. Just get here quickly.
Me: Why didn't you call me when you arrived?

I begin gathering my stuff, trying not to disturb the rest of the class as I make my exit. I walk to my car—or Vance's, technically. Adriano had to do something this morning and told me Vance said I could drive myself. But something about this feels wrong.

Vance: I'm in the middle of something. I'll call you soon. Just get here quickly.

I sigh. I'm just being paranoid over seeing my father again and what this visit may entail. My body hums with nervous energy as I climb behind the wheel. I send a quick text off to Brix to tell her to check on Samson. That I have a family emergency.

Brix: Do you need me to come with you?

Me: No, Vance is meeting me.

Brix: Keep me updated. If I don't hear from you by tonight, I'm coming to find you.

I smile to myself. Loving how protective she is of me. Always ready to fight for me. And I her. I have the scar to prove it. I press Play on Lana Del Rey's "Born to Die" and begin driving.

I PULL UP TO MY OLD CHILDHOOD HOME, QUICKLY CLIMBING OUT. I leave my things behind as I rush to the front door, ringing the doorbell. The fact that Vance has me coming here must mean it's something important. I would let myself in but I threw my key away as soon as I moved out. I never planned to come back. My father opens the door, his mouth set in a frown, eyes confused as his eyebrows pull down. "Primrose, what are you—" Father's eyes widen and his knees give in as he falls to the floor.

I gasp, "Father?" I reach down to help him, when something smacks me in the back of the head. My vision darkens and I fall on top of my father.

VANCE

My phone rings and I make a motion with my hand for them to turn the chainsaw off. I've been up and down the country, torturing different branches of the Outfit. Surprise, no one knows anything about the hit on my wife's head. They've heard of it, but everyone swears they would never. Like the fucker who is currently about to lose his leg for not talking. "Hello?"

"Vance, how is Prim?" Brixley asks into the phone, her voice deep in worry. "I have this bad feeling in my stomach, and I can't reach her. She said you were meeting her at her father's house?"

My stomach sinks. "Why would she think that?" I always try to stay calm until I know all the details but when it involves my wife, there is no calm in a single molecule of my body.

Brixley goes quiet. "She said you were meeting her there. Are you not there?"

"When did she leave?" I begin jogging to my rental car.

"Around noon. Are you saying you are not with her?"

"That's what I'm fucking saying." I hit End on the call with my sister and call Adriano, who doesn't pick up. "Worthless," I growl into the phone.

I call and arrange the private jet. There is no way I'll make it to her father's house before one in the morning in this car and the situation is dire at this point.

FUCK.

I pull up to the Thatcher house, my Range Rover parked in the driveway. I release a breath and climb out. I don't even knock, I just open the door. Mr. Thatcher peeks around the corner and sighs when he sees me.

"Where is my wife?" My voice is so sharp and dull I barely recognize it.

"I... I saw her but then I was knocked out."

I grind my teeth, grabbing him by his shirt and slamming him into the wall. I hold my pistol under his chin. He shakes like a leaf, but I couldn't give two fucks. "Tell me everything. And if you leave a single detail out, I'll have you repenting until I send you to your precious God."

23
PRIMROSE

Make. It. Stop.

I squint my eyes into the cold room. There is a single light hanging from the ceiling. There are no walls, just metal bars on each side of the room. I pull on my wrists but only hear the clank of metal as they stay bound above me. I try to swallow but my mouth is dry, my head pounds and aches.

The cell door swings open and black heels come into view. My eyes trail up the black pencil skirt and stop on the solid white mask. The smile pulled into something far too happy and creepy. The eyes are black and nonexistent. The mask tilts its face. "You're awake," a soft female voice says. "Good."

I don't respond, but I scoot back as much as I can. I'm oddly calm. I feel numb. Whatever this is, there is nothing I can do to stop it. My mind tells me my husband finally got tired of me, but my heart knows this is not him. I've been set up.

"This is nothing personal to you. It's the vile man you

married. You can thank him for this." She takes a step closer. "Don't be scared, you won't die today or even tomorrow. This is just a little message for your husband." She turns, and a man enters.

His mask is also white, but the expression isn't happy, it's a crying face and he seems hesitant as he steps up to me, unbuckling his pants. The calm washes and I scoot farther into the brick wall of the cell. He latches his hands around my ankles, pulling me against the concrete floor, scraping up my thighs. *God, please, no.* I kick at him, but he puts each of my ankles in chains, stretching my body. I shake my head. "Please, don't," I plead.

He grunts, cutting up my dress. It feels like I can feel my heart break when he puts a condom on. I feel so hopeless. There is nothing I can do to stop the situation and what is about to happen. He grabs my neck and whispers, "You'll thank me later." And then he presses down until my vision fades.

I MOAN, SQUEEZING MY EYES TO KEEP THEM SHUT, HOPING THE darkness keeps me under longer. Something moves inside of me and my stomach rolls. *Please, no.* In between my thighs it feels raw, aching with each thrust. I can feel something slowly dripping down my legs. "Please," I whisper, opening my eyes. "Knock me out," I beg.

The masked man chuckles. "Wish I could, but that's not what the boss wants." He throws his head back, and acid burns in my throat as he groans with his release. Tears coats my cheeks as he climbs off, tossing the condom to the side and zipping up his pants.

I look to the pile of condoms next to me and I do throw up, the acidic liquid rolling down my chin. It's only bile because I don't have any food in my stomach.

"Next," the woman says, and another white mask comes in.

I don't even look at his mask as he enters me roughly. As my body moves across the concrete with each thrust, I look to the ceiling, growing numb. I feel them move in me, grabbing my breasts roughly, saliva covering my cheek from some of the men that spat on me. My tears dry, my mind calms. The lady looks down at me in her white smiling mask. "We're almost done."

I don't say anything as the next three tear through me. I simply just drift off to somewhere else.

THE CELL DOOR FINALLY CLOSES, THE CHATTER DYING OUT AS THEY walk away. I lift my head to look at my body. Blue and purple bruises litter my breasts. Dry, crusty blood on my thighs. My dress lays dingy and torn around my body.

This didn't happen. This is a bad dream.

I refuse to look over at the pile of condoms, I don't want to know how many men there was. *It doesn't matter, because this never happened,* my brain whispers, and I close my eyes. My body aches. I'm sore between my legs. My breasts feel abused, and my mind is so tired. So fucking tired.

The cell door opens again and I jump. The hair on my body rising as I get ready for the next attack. The white mask with the crying face walks in, looking at his feet. He unties my body from the chains. My arms feel heavy and drop to the floor. He ties my arms and legs with rope before throwing my limp body over his shoulder.

"Tell your husband to reject the leadership position."

And then he tosses my body into the back seat of a car.

My body hits the rough ground at the entrance to our home. The iron gate digs into my side as I try to wiggle myself free from the rope. A car stops close to my body, the tires screeching loud as I hear a door open. I flinch away as hands touch me. "Hey, it's okay," Madden whispers.

I hear Amiyah crying loudly as Madden picks me up. "Why the fuck does this keep happening?" she sobs.

"Amiyah, calm down," Madden says gently, climbing into the back seat with me as Amiyah pulls through the driveway. "We were just coming over to come up with a plan to find you," he says, shaking his head.

My throat hurts as I let the tears fall freely. A small cry of pain and relief settles in the back of my throat.

The door opens and Madden says calmly, "You need to get a doctor over here quickly. And take the girls to another room before I bring her in."

"Fuck," Beckett says, his words filled with emotion as he drapes his jacket over me. "Vance is going to set the world on fire when he sees her."

"Where is he?"

"On his way."

Madden lifts me gently with him as he climbs out of the car. He takes me inside and upstairs to the room I share with Vance, then places me on the bed. "You can't take a shower. Any evidence can't be washed away, but let's get you some clothes, yeah?"

I nod, pointing to Vance's drawer. I want to be wrapped in him so I can feel safe. Madden smiles a little when he sees it's Vance's stuff that I want to wear right now. He places a shirt and sweatpants on the bed. "Do you want me to help you? Do you want me to go get the girls or be alone?"

"Girls, please," I whisper.

He nods. "I'll be back."

Madden leaves and I look down at my hands and watch them shake. The door swings open and a small gasp greets me, but I just keep staring at my hands until my vision is blurred with tears.

"Hey, love." Amiyah touches me and I flinch away from her. Looking up, I see her face is contorted in pain as her lips tremble. "I'm sorry, I'll ask before I touch you."

I shake my head. "It's fine," I whisper.

"Come on, Prim. Let's get you changed," Brixley says softly.

Brixley and Amiyah help strip me of what's left of my clothes and help me put on Vance's. I sit back on the bed as a knock sounds on the door. A woman walks in, a kind smile on her face as she carries a huge bag and rolls in a machine. "Hello, Primrose. I'm Doctor Fisher."

The girls rise and I grip their hands, eyes pleading for them to stay. Amiyah closes the door and comes to sit back with Brixley and me.

"I'm going to apologize in advance, but I have to use a rape kit on you. See if we can get any DNA as to who did this."

"It was multiple men."

The doctor's eyes shine but she looks away quickly, asking me to take off my sweats as she sets everything up. Amiyah distracts me as the doctor swabs down there. "Okay, now I'm going to do an ultrasound to see if everything is okay in your uterus, is that okay?" I nod.

She uses a wand-like thing and it hurts as she inserts it inside me. She looks to the screen and her eyes widen. "It would have been helpful if you told me you were pregnant."

"What?" I ask, my heart speeding up.

"You didn't know?" the doctor asks.

"No, of course not. I'm on birth control..." I shake my head.

"Birth control is not always accurate." The doctor says just as chaos breaks outside the door.

I hear a loud crash outside the room in the hall. "You need to wait until the doctor is done," Beckett says.

"Fuck that and you. Move," Vance growls.

I smile. "My husband is home."

"Everything looks okay, baby's heart rate is good. No trauma there. The blood on your legs is from the tearing. Physically you are fine, but as for your mental health, I suggest you see someone, Primrose. And an OB-GYN. You look to be close to three months along, so you need to be on prenatal vitamins." The doctor packs her things.

"Did she say baby?" Brixley asks.

"I think so," Amiyah whispers.

"Shit," I say.

"Are you going to tell him?" Brixley whispers.

I nod. "Maybe later, though."

The door swings open and Vance stops in the doorway, jaw tightening. "Everyone out."

No one says a word as they leave and shut the door

behind them. Vance covers his mouth with his hand. Staring at me as he walks to my side of the bed. I sit up, wincing slightly. Vance drops to his knees. His arms going around my waist as he lays his head in my lap. "I'm so fucking sorry, Angel."

I run my hands through his thick hair, holding my tears back. He lifts his face from my lap, pulling the covers back. Gently, he picks me up, cradling me to his chest as he walks us to the bathroom. He punches buttons on the controller, and I watch as the shower room begins to fill with steam. He sits me on the counter, his fingers tugging on the hem of my shirt. I hold the shirt down, shaking my head. He grinds his teeth. "Let me see." I shake my head again, more stupid tears falling. "Baby," he cups my cheeks, "no matter what, I will stay calm. I will never see you as anything other than my beautiful wife." He drops his hands to the shirt and tugs. "Now, let me see."

I close my eyes as he lifts the shirt. I know what he's seeing, why he's silent as rage fills the room with tension. "Who did this?" he asks quietly.

"I don't know," I whisper, opening my eyes.

Vance's throat works and his eyes shine as he stares down at me. I cup his cheeks, bringing his eyes back to mine. "Get in the shower with me. I don't want to be alone."

He nods, stepping back to take off his clothes. He picks me up and my legs wrap around his waist as I lay my head on his inked chest. He walks us into the shower and leans against the tile wall. He looks down at me in his arms, lowering his head to take my mouth gently. Happy tears fall down my cheeks, dripping over our lips. I'm relieved to be in his safety again. The fact that he is willing to still kiss me, touch me after I've been so used up by others. I know he doesn't know all the details but he's not stupid. So the fact that he can still look at me, touch me, protect me, makes me feel so content—for now.

He pulls back, opening his mouth, but I shake my head. "I'll tell you everything tomorrow."

24
PRIMROSE

I'VE HAD A LONG MORNING. Recounting every detail I could remember to Vance as he listened. Emotions turned off. He was like a robot. As if I'm not his wife recounting an assault of rape to him. When I was finished, he nodded his head once and then took off, but I heard the rage coming from his office. The sound of things smashing against the wall.

I went to my sewing room, where I've stayed holed up in since. Working on a skirt. Listing to the hum of the machine. Sewing has always eased my mind, kept me busy. It's the perfect distraction. And I think I deserve that right now. Between what I went through to finding out I'm carrying a child. I place my hand over my still flat stomach. How do I even tell my husband he's going to be a father? Do you give mafia princes cute little picture frames with a sonagram? I shake my head, rising from my sewing machine and leaving the room. I walk down the hall, stopping at the spare bathroom and grabbing a first aid kit. Slowly, I push open the door to Vance's office. "Honey?"

I see Vance in his desk chair, a glass of whiskey in his hand, room destroyed as he levels me with a flat look. I step over the shattered glass and broken wood, take a seat on his desk in front of him, and open the first aid kit.

"Hands," I say, holding mine out.

He rolls his eyes, putting his glass down and holding up his hands. I pause, bringing the split knuckles closer. I place both hands together. His once blank knuckles are now covered in bold ink. *Primrose*. I look up to catch him watching me. "You got my name tattooed on your knuckles?"

He nods. "I told you I was saving them for something special."

My chest swells and my lips break out into a smile. "You got this done while you were gone?"

He nods. "One day away and I was missing you. Decided I wanted to carry you with me forever."

I swallow thickly. Clearing my throat, I grab a cotton ball and pour some rubbing alcohol on it. I begin dabbing his bloodied knuckles. Not able to look at him. This is huge, right?

I hear the door swing open behind me and Vance moves quickly. "Where the fuck where you?" he seethes.

"I—" The voice cuts off in a mumble and I turn quickly to see Vance has placed his gun in Adriano's mouth.

I hop down off the desk and walk over to them slowly, placing a hand on Vance's arm. "Vance," I whisper.

He looks down at me, jaw ticking. He removes the gun but sends Adriano to the ground with a fist in his gut. Adriano wheezes at Vance's feet. "I trusted you with her and look what happened."

Adriano nods, but I softly repeat, "Vance."

"Don't protect me, Primrose. I failed at my job. He has every right to punish me."

Vance laughs. "You'll be praying for punishment when I

get done with you. You let the only thing on this entire earth I care about get hurt. You'll be lucky if you fucking live." Vance looks at me. "Amiyah will be here soon. Something about a checkup with the doctor." He leans down, kissing me.

"Primrose!" Amiyah sings through the house.

I sigh, looking back to Vance. "Go," he says gently.

"Amiyah, where are we going? I don't have a checkup."

She throws her car into park and turns to look at me. "I scheduled you an appointment. We need to check on my godchild you're growing. Out. Don't want to be late."

Amiyah rushes me into the waiting room, checking me in as I sit nervously on a chair. Why am I nervous? She sits beside me, a clipboard in her hand. "Name? Primrose De Luca," she writes. "Birthday? Easy." She smiles, going through my basics. "Last period?" She looks over to me.

"I have no clue."

She clicks her tongue, shaking her head. "Unknown. Family history... Do you—"

"Give me that." I snatch the clipboard and finish answering the rest of the questions by the time my name is called.

"Primrose?" a nurse calls. She has on light pink scrubs and a huge smile.

I take a deep breath. Amiyah is the first to the door. "Amiyah, godmother," she introduces herself.

The nurse blinks rapidly at her and then smiles. "Nurse Becky, and you must be Primrose?" she asks me.

"I am. It's a pleasure to meet you."

Nurse Becky takes my weight and blood pressure and then I'm led into a room. "Here is a gown to change into and Doctor Peterson will be in shortly."

Amiyah smiles at me and I sigh. "A little heads-up would have been nice."

"But then you would have not come." She shrugs.

I put the gown on and lay the cover over my lower half. Doctor Peterson walks in, introducing herself. She's very impersonal and gets straight to business. "Here is the baby's heartbeat." My eyes well up as I watch the tiny bean move and kick around on the screen. Hear the rapid thumps of my baby's heart beating, and it causes an overwhelming bliss to wrap around me.

"Oh my god, there is a baby inside me." I hiccup, smiling.

"Look at my little godbaby," Amiyah coos, wiping her cheeks.

"Very healthy baby. Good heartbeat, movement is strong," the doctor says, clicking a few buttons, and some pictures print out from the machine. "I want to see you back in four weeks and by then, we will be able to tell what the gender is." She removes her gloves and helps me sit up. "Any concerns?"

I shake my head. The doctor smiles and nods. "Good. I'll see you soon, Primrose." She hands the pictures to Amiyah.

"We have to do a cute little announcement for Vance. I can't wait to see the look of horror on his face."

My face falls and I start to cry. "Oh, shit," Amiyah hisses. "It's going to be fine. He will be so happy once he gets used to the idea. Shh, love. I'm sorry."

"It's all too much." I sniff.

"It really is but you've got this. You are the strongest

person I know, Primrose. You're going to be one hell of a mother."

"You think?" I ask, blinking the tears away.

"Positive. Now, come on. Let's get you dressed, and I'll get you some pickles and ice cream. Whatever my godchild wants."

I laugh, wiping my tears away. Once I'm dressed, I look down at my sonograms.

I'm having a baby.

I YAWN, STRETCHING IN OUR BED. VANCE CALLED AND TOLD ME TO come back home as soon as I was done with my checkup. When I got home, he had dinner ready, but the smell made me puke, so instead he took me to bed, giving me my outlaw romance book as he answered phone calls. Samson curled up into my lap as I read until finally, I fell asleep.

I grab my robe, pulling it on as I get the pictures out of my purse and gently put them in my pocket. I follow the smell of pancakes and find Vance at the table, sipping coffee. He looks up, but quickly looks away. I frown.

"Hey," I say. "I need to talk to you about something."

He sets his mug down, standing with a thick stack of papers in his hand. "So do I." He lays the papers gently in front of me, but I don't look at them. Instead, I look to him as he hands me a pen. "Can you sign those for me?"

"What are they?" I ask.

"Divorce papers."

25
VANCE

"No," she says, shocked. She stands, eyes shining as she looks at me with disbelief. And it fucking guts me. I reach for her, but she smacks my hands away. "I don't understand," she whispers brokenly.

"I promised to protect you, and I've failed. Multiple times. My world, the world I will have to force you to live in, it's... it's not that you're not strong enough to live in it, Primrose. It's that I'm not strong enough to live if something happens to you."

A single tear falls from her eye and my hand twitches with the need to wipe it away. "Is that not my decision to make? How can you make a decision that affects both of our lives?" She takes a step back, her lip trembling.

I have to push through. This is what is best for her. "No. It's mine. When it comes to you being in my life or you being safe, I'll chose your safety every time." I step toward her.

"But your title?"

"I'll marry someone I don't care about."

"So, you're choosing the mafia over me?" She clutches

her chest as if she's in pain and I want to take it all back, but I can't. This is the only way to keep her safe.

"Yes." That's all it takes to watch her break. She leans against the couch, tears falling as she stares at me as if she doesn't even know who I am anymore. *I'm sorry, Angel.*

"Do you not love me?" she whispers.

I close my eyes as pain shoots through my chest, cutting through every fiber of my being and burning me alive. "Of fucking course, I do. Why do you think I'm doing all of this?" I grab her waist, pulling her to me. One hand in her hair as I tip her head back so I can stare into her glacier eyes one more time. Permanently ink the image to my brain forever.

"Promise me you'll move on. With a good guy this time. Not a bastard like me but one whose world doesn't revolve around crime." Every word feels like lead. I don't want her to move the fuck on without me. "Find someone who isn't damaged. Someone who doesn't give a fuck about some silly scar on your face that you earned with honor. Find someone who loves you so much he'll burn the world to the fucking ground for hurting you. You hear me, Primrose?" I close my eyes and rest my forehead against hers, breathing in her scent as my oxygen. Nothing has ever hurt like this.

"But most importantly, hate me, Angel. Hate me for thinking I could have you. Hate me for loving you more than I care to breathe." My voice lowers as I lower my lips to hers and whisper, "Just hate me."

She shakes her head and I kiss her. I kiss her long and hard, savoring her taste and running my tongue over every inch of her lips. I kiss her so long she grows weak in my arms and when I move away, she desperately holds on to me. "Please," she whispers, face wet with tears, eyes pleading.

I shake my head, stepping back. "Sign the papers, Angel."

She looks away, walking to the table. With trembling fingers, she signs the papers and sits the pen down. She won't look at me as she says, "So what? We're supposed to go to the same college, have the same friends, and not be with each other?"

I swallow. "I'm leaving, Primrose. I'm done with school. You can have everything. The cars, the house. The only thing I can't give you is me, baby."

"That's the only thing I want," she says dejectedly, walking away without a backward glance.

When she reaches the stairs, I stop her. "What did you want to tell me?"

She shakes her head. "It doesn't matter anymore."

And I watch as my entire world walks away. But a man like me, we don't deserve a world as beautiful as her.

"Thanks, man," I say to Madden as he loads the last of Primrose's things. I know she left a lot here, because the house is in her name, but she doesn't want to stay here right now. She's going back to The Misfits' house.

Madden shakes his head. "I think you're making a mistake."

"Yeah, well." I shrug. "Can't keep her safe. Maybe eliminating myself will."

"You're a fucking idiot." He slams the car door in my face, and I watch as he drives away. I climb into my own car, starting it up. I still have business to attend to. Like figuring out who hurt my angel.

26
PRIMROSE

A MONTH later

There is a knock on the door of my old room at The Misfits' house. My eyes are crusted shut from tears and I can't stop throwing up to save my life. I clutch my small swollen belly and begin to cry again.

"Prim, how are you feeling?" Brixley asks, sitting on my bed and pushing my hair out of my face.

"Horrible. Your niece or nephew is sucking the life out of me."

She frowns. "Is that normal?" she ask.

I sigh. "I don't know. I've never done this before." We're both quiet for a moment. "Have you talked to him?" I whisper.

Brixley shakes her head. "No, and I wouldn't answer if he called. It's been a month and I know you love him or whatever but it's time you stop crying all the time."

"It's mainly the hormones. I can't help it," I lie.

Brixley sighs. "I know. But good news. You get to find out the gender of your baby today. Amiyah has been going on and on about it all morning. She can't wait to take you.

She's calling herself your baby daddy." I laugh, my nose wrinkling. "Also, Nick, the guy you recruited? He didn't make it through the trials."

I frown. "It's only the first one."

Brixley shrugs. "Kid doesn't trust anyone."

Beckett took over my recruit with everything going on. I kind of knew Nick wouldn't make it if Beckett was in charge, but I didn't have much choice. "Well, that sucks," I say.

Brixley nods. "Now, go get ready. We are all eager to know what our Misfit baby is." She smiles, patting my leg.

I grab my phone, but I only have a text from Amiyah in all caps that it's baby day. Nothing from *him*, though. Our divorce was finalized yesterday. Somehow, he got it rushed and over with. It was almost as quick as our marriage. He didn't even show up to the lawyer's office. He just left me the house, his cars, and a ton of money.

I groan, rising to stand and rubbing my belly. I'm not big yet but because I'm so small, I'm already showing. Hiding under thick clothes has been my go-to so far.

Madden thinks I should tell Vance. Maybe I should but it's not like he's reached out.

"It's just you, me, and The Misfits, baby," I tell my stomach, grabbing some clothes.

AMIYAH CLUTCHES THE WHITE ENVELOPE TO HER CHEST THAT HAS the baby's gender in it. Brixley tries to snatch it. "Sorry, Brix. I'm the godmother, so only I know."

Brixley puts her hands on her hips. "Well, I'm the aunt."

"That doesn't matter. I have mother in my name," Amiyah says.

"I'm the actual mother," I chime in.

"Stay out of this, Prim," Brixley tells me.

I shake my head, walking to the kitchen, but pause as I listen.

"You can get fucked," Beckett says into the phone. A pause, and then, "No, you can't come to fucking Thanksgiving. If it were up to me, I would kick your ass out of The Misfits." Beckett growls, "You will not come here parading your new fiancée around her. Your divorce was finalized yesterday, and you announce today you have a new fiancée?"

I gasp, my legs crumbling. Beckett turns, eyes wide as he whispers, "Shit."

I clutch the bar, my eyes stinging. "He has a new fiancée?" I ask. "It's only been a day."

"No," Beckett says sharply into the phone. "I've got to go." Beckett walks over to me. "Are you okay?"

I throw up on his shoes.

"Why are we outside in the dark?" I ask, my stomach aching and mind so tired. I just want to go to sleep for a week.

Amiyah directs me to a chair, and I sit in it as the rest of them sit around me in chairs. "Look to the sky," Amiyah says, and I do just as fireworks begin to go off. *It's a boy!* surrounded by bright blue twinkling lights illuminate the sky.

"Oh my god." I giggle, my eyes wide and my heart so

warm for the first time in so long. Everyone cheers as blue lights flicker to life and the back porch is decorated in blue streamers with a giant cake. Tons of snacks and blue drinks. The firepit lit with blue flames, and I find myself crying again.

Beckett blows out a breath. "I really thought she would like this."

"I do," I say, "these are happy tears."

Brixley and Amiyah grab me in a hug, jumping up and down around me. And I'm so happy that my ex-husband's engagement slips my mind. For now.

27
VANCE

Two months later

Arms wrap around my neck from behind and I grind my teeth. "Don't touch me."

She laughs, the voice like nails on a chalkboard. "Fine, maybe you want to touch me?"

I spin, taking in the half-dressed woman I'm going to be married to soon spreading her legs open seductively. "Not in this life."

"If you don't, I'll have to find someone who will."

I nod. "You should and while you're at it, let him fill you up with babies, move in with him. I don't fucking care. This is an arrangement with no benefits. You can do nothing to change that."

She pouts, trailing her hands over her breasts. "Nothing?"

"Fucking nothing. Now get out of my room."

She huffs, standing and walking out with what little dignity she has left as I look down at my phone. It's been three months since I've seen or spoken to my angel. Holidays have come and gone. Which I was forced to spend with my family since Beckett refuses to allow me to visit them. I get it and respect him for it, but I just want a little glimpse. No one has posted a single picture with Primrose in it. My mother won't even look at me when I come home.

Everyone is isolating me, and I deserve it.

But I fucking miss her. Miss her random facts, her sweet laugh. I miss her gentleness, how she sighs lightly when she wakes up. How her eyes flutter when I run my finger over her scar. I miss her blue glacier eyes and the way they light up when I walk into a room. But most of all, I miss her touch. Not just in a sexual way either. The hugs, the tiny touches to my bicep. Her fingers combing through my hair.

I stand, frustrated, thinking of making a rash decision like going to her and apologizing, but I can't. I fucking can't.

But fuck, I wish I could.

PRIMROSE

I rub my swollen belly, groaning. "Please get out of my ribs, little boy. You're hurting Momma." I'm six, almost seven months pregnant now and I'm starting not to be able to see my feet. This child is huge already, not that I'm surprised. I walk up the steps to Vance's parents' house. I made the decision to let them know. This is their grandchild, and this will be my baby's only grandparents.

I ring the doorbell, my jacket not quiet hiding my belly anymore. Vance's mom opens the door smiling, shock covering her face. "Primrose..." Her eyes fall to my stomach. "Oh my god," she gasps, her hand reaching out and touching my bump. "Is it..." she trails off.

"Yes."

"Does he know? My gosh, how far along are you?"

I shake my head. "He doesn't know, and I'm almost seven months along."

"But you've only been split up three months," she says, smiling at my stomach as her eyes water.

"I know," I say softly. "The day I was going to tell him, he handed me divorce papers."

His mother's face hardens. "He's an idiot," she says, taking my hand. "Come inside."

"I'm not ready to tell him. I'm still hurt."

"Sorry, darling. But it's a little too late for that." Vance's father comes into the living room as I take my jacket off. "He just pulled up."

I freeze, panicking. "I could go out the back door?"

He smiles. "Sure. Whatever you want, Primrose."

I pause, and then I shake my head, grabbing my jacket and walking quickly to the back door. "Where is she?" Vance's voice booms through the house.

"Not sure," his dad responds. "Sweetheart, have you seen *her*?" he asks his wife.

"Tell my son I haven't." I throw open the back door, not bothering to close it, and sneak around the house.

I'm about to turn around the corner to reach the front of the house, when a hand reaches out, grabbing my neck and pulling me back toward the house. "Got you, Angel," Vance whispers in my ear.

"Be gentle with her, son. If you hurt my future grandchild, I may have to kill you," Vance's dad says from behind him.

Vance looks confused, and when he looks at my stomach, his eyes widen and shoot back to mine. "What the fuck, Angel."

"Surprise," I say weakly and push on his chest.

He takes a step back, hands on his hips as he stares at

my stomach. A woman walks up beside him, smiling viciously at me. "What's going on, Vancey?" Her engagement ring flashes on her left hand and I stiffen. But then I find my inner Brixley and tilt my chin up.

"I need to get going," I say.

Vance's mom comes running. "Wait," she calls out. "I'll make them leave. Please just come inside," she pleads.

"Yes, Primrose," his father says. "Come in. I'll get rid of the unwanted guests. Plus, I have dinner already prepared. For the three of us," he adds sternly.

I bite my lip, looking to a still shocked Vance and his new fiancée and back to my child's grandparents. "Okay," I nod, taking Aurora's arm.

"Can everyone hold on for one goddamn minute?" Vance says.

"I'm so confused. Who even is she?" his fiancée asks.

"Shut the fuck up," Vance snaps. "Primrose, come here for a fucking minute."

I shake my head. "I'm good. Enjoy your evening."

We leave Vance and his fiancée outside with his father as his mom fusses over me. Asking me questions about the health of my son. If I need somewhere to stay, would I stay here for a few weeks after the baby is born. I politely decline, but I promise to keep her updated and that she can come to the next appointment with me. After the meal, I drive myself back home to my family—The Misfits. Except, it's not just my family, it's his too—and he's here. Waiting on the front steps for me.

28
VANCE

A BABY.

She's been carrying my baby and didn't even fucking tell me. I knock on the door to The Misfits' house—the code has been changed, apparently, and when Brixley opens the door, she glares and then firmly shuts it in my face. "Open up, Soulless." I pound on the door.

"Eat shit," she yells back.

I sigh, taking a seat on the steps, and watch the sun fall behind the trees. Waiting until I see a car pull in. I rise, my body humming with nervous energy. When I was told she was heading to my parents' house today, I flipped my car around. I was supposed to have dinner with my future in-laws, but I couldn't miss the chance to see her. I just wanted a glimpse, but something overpowered me. I didn't just want to see her, I wanted to touch her. No matter how cruel it was for either of us.

But then, I saw her bump and my mind went to mush.

Primrose climbs out of the car, her hand firmly on her swollen stomach as she walks toward the house. I shove my hands in my pockets to keep from reaching out and grabbing her. When she gets closer, I ask, "Can we talk, please?"

She nods, walking past me. "Sure. Come on."

I follow behind her far too closely. Taking in her scent and tempted to touch the silken strands of her hair. She punches in the code and walks in the door. I follow like a lost dog after her, coming face to face with my old friends, who are scowling at me.

Primrose sits her bag down on the entryway before turning to face everyone. "I'm going to talk to Vance in my room. I expect you won't be listening through the door?"

No one says a word and it makes me almost smirk. Primrose exhales, climbing up the stairs and leading me to her own room. She tosses her jacket to the chair, sitting on the bed, and groans in relief as she takes her shoes off. I take a seat at her vanity, my leg bouncing nervously as she looks up to me. "Let's talk. Should we start with how you divorced me two days after I was raped?" I flinch. "Or how you broke me the first time you told me you love me?" I open my mouth, but her voice rises. "Or how you never fucking called to see how I was doing?" She points to her stomach. "Or how about this? Which wound will you pick first?"

Her cheeks are flushed with anger as she stands, going to her drawer and pulling out soft pajamas. I divert my eyes as she starts to change in front of me. "I was only trying to protect you," I say.

She laughs harshly at that. "And yet here you are, back in my life."

"You're carrying my baby," I grind out, checking my temper.

"Doesn't mean you have to come back into our lives."

I stand, walking over to her and tipping her chin up.

"Then what does it mean?" I look between her eyes. *Fuck, I missed these. Missed her.*

She hardens her eyes. "It means, sign your rights away and be done with us."

"Fucking never," I growl. "You think I'm done with you?" I laugh, moving my face closer to hers. "You were never going to escape me."

She swallows. "I have divorce papers that say I have."

I laugh louder. "A piece of paper can't stop me."

Her lips tremble. "Well, I don't want you anymore."

"Too fucking bad." I let go of her and walk to the door. "You either move back home or I move in." I open the door and Brixley and Amiyah fall inside. I shake my head as I step over them.

"She's never going to forgive you," Amiyah whispers as she trails after me.

We'll fucking see about that.

BOTH OF THESE WALL PAINTS LOOK EXACTLY THE SAME. I HOLD them up in the light to see if I can tell the difference between them. Nope, still the fucking same. "I can't tell them apart," I sigh.

Beckett peers over my shoulder. "You're going with black? For a baby room. Really?"

"Are you a baby whisper? Why does it matter what color the walls are painted?"

Beckett shrugs and Madden walks over. "That one," he points to the left paint sample. "Has more gray tones while the other only has black." I level him with a flat look. "I'd go with the gray tones."

"Fine. And, Beckett, I choose black because it's gender neutral."

Beckett smirks. "She didn't tell you the gender?"

I pause, raising an eyebrow. "Do you know?"

He nods. "Yep. Had a big-ass gender reveal."

My jaw tics. "And?"

"I hope it favors Primrose over your ugly mug."

"Fucking unbelievable," I mumble, walking to the counter and demanding midnight, shade forty. There are fifty-one shades of midnight, apparently. The guys and I load up the paint and drop it off at my house.

"I think you're getting ahead of yourself," Madden supplies. "Primrose won't even look at you."

No fucking shit. I went over there early to bring her a stupid hot chocolate, which Amiyah informed me she can't drink anymore because it makes her nauseous. The little witch then proceeded to make Primrose a cup of hot tea and toast. Glaring at me as she made it. And when my angel came down the stairs, she ignored me. As if I wasn't sitting right next to her. I knew she wouldn't be jumping into my arms, but now that we have a child in the mix, I thought we could act like adults.

I pull up to The Misfits' home, a familiar car in the driveway. I throw mine into park, climbing out and going inside. My mother's laughter rings and I find her and Primrose in the living room. I cross my arms, leaning against the doorframe, a smile lifting my lips as I watch them.

My mom's hand rubs Primrose's swollen belly and something close to jealousy hits me. I want to touch her, feel our child kicking in her stomach. "Oh." My mother laughs. "My grandbaby is kicking." She laughs again, wiping a happy tear from her cheek. "Well, let's get going, we have lots of shopping to do. Plus, my husband will be meeting us. He surprisingly has lots of opinions on baby clothes." My mother shrugs and Primrose laughs, her face lighting up.

They both pause when they see me. "Where are you going?"

My mother narrows her eyes, and Primrose sighs. "Baby clothes shopping. Would you like to come?"

I nod. "I would."

She gives me a fake smile. "Okay, well, let's go."

My father didn't end up meeting us; he came by and drove us instead, which forced Primrose and I in the back seat together. Primrose rubs her temple with one hand, her other resting on her bump. "Are you okay?" I ask gently.

"I just have a headache." She closes her eyes.

I reach my hand over to the back of her head, massaging her scalp, and she sighs, leaning into me. "You two should get comfortable, the drive will be a little long."

My mom and dad chat quietly in the front seat as I work my fingers against my angel's scalp. Her body grows limp, and her head falls closer and closer until her head is resting on my shoulder, her eyes closed in sleep. I stare down at her bump. Can't believe I missed so much already. I reach my hand out gently, laying it on her stomach. Invading her boundaries like I've always done. I rest my head on hers, rubbing gentle circles on her stomach.

"Son," my mother speaks softly. I look up to her. "I got rid of your fiancée for you. You're welcome. Now, try and get my real daughter back." She turns around and I close my eyes.

Easier said than done.

MY EYES FLY OPEN AS SOMETHING BUMPS INTO MY HAND. I look down to my hand still resting on Primrose's bump. Primrose giggles softly. "He's active today."

"He?" I ask, still mesmerized by the fact that the baby is kicking me.

"Yeah. Our baby is a boy."

"Name?" I ask.

I feel her shake her head against my shoulder. "I haven't chosen one. I want to see his face first. But I like the name Storm."

I chuckle. "That's such a rich person thing of you to do."

"Storm De Luca has a nice ring to it, though, don't you agree?"

"Sounds very powerful," I admit, the name growing on me the longer I think about it.

Primrose suddenly jerks up, moving away from me. "Sorry, I didn't mean to fall asleep on you."

Why does that hurt? Her apologizing to me for sleeping peacefully in my arms? "Apologizing is something you'll never have to do with me, Angel. No matter how much you think you messed up."

The car comes to a stop in front of a huge three-story mall. "We're here," my mom singsongs, she and Primrose climbing out quickly.

"Son." I pause at my father's voice, meeting his eyes in the review mirror. "Keep trying."

What the fuck does he think I am doing?

29
PRIMROSE

I MISS AMIYAH AND BRIXLEY. Ever since I moved back in with Vance, it's been so quiet. I go to school, then come home and have an awkward dinner with my ex-husband. I can see he's trying but it was so easy for him to toss me away. Act as if I never existed.

I go downstairs, making my tea and going to the back porch. Samson meows, almost tripping me as he curls around my legs. "Careful," I murmur to my sassy cat. We both walk outside, and I pause, my cup slipping from my hands and shattering on the stone porch. Samson hisses, ducking back in the house. I hiccup and then give in to a sob as I stare at the dead kitten on my porch.

"Primrose," Vance yells, and I turn around to see him in only a pair of sweats and his gun in his hand. "What's going on?" he asks, frantically checking our surroundings.

I sniff. "There is a dead kitten."

He pauses, raising his eyebrows at me. "A dead kitten?" I nod, stepping back to let him see it. He sighs, setting the gun inside and walking back out. "It's just a cat, Primrose. He probably..." I begin to sob, loudly. "Shit."

Vance wraps his arms around me and I burry my face in his chest. "I'll buy you a hundred kittens if you just stop crying, Angel."

"I..." I stammer. "All I do is cry and grow fat. My feet hurt, my breasts hurt, my back hurts, and your son won't move his feet from my ribs." He chuckles and I run my hands down his abs. "It's not funny."

"It's a little funny."

I groan. "Vance, please stop touching me."

"Why?"

"Because you're extremely beautiful and I haven't had anyone touch me in months, not to mention, these hormones make me so horny and, well, please, just stop touching me."

"And miss the opportunity to sink deep inside your honey-soaked pussy? Not a fucking chance," he growls by my ear.

"We have too much we need to fix."

"Yeah, I have a lot to fix when it comes to you, but I can fix this one now."

I groan. "No, we can't." I pull away from him, even though it feels nice to be in his arms. But this man broke me. Left me when I needed him most. Freaking divorced me. "How can we ever be anything but co-parents? We need to talk about the baby. Where will he sleep? Will we live with you for the first few months or maybe you'll just come help?" I shake my head.

"What do you mean co-parents?" He steps closer to me.

"I mean, you will be a part of this baby's life, but not mine." I tilt my chin up.

"Oh, yeah?" He steps closer, invading my personal space with his manly scent of whiskey and coffee. "Then what are you doing here?" He places a hand on my bump, rubbing softly. "Because it looks to me like if you didn't really want anything to do with me, you wouldn't be here."

I tremble beneath his touch "You didn't give me a choice."

"That's an excuse and we both know it. Admit it, Angel. You still love me."

I shake my head. "I have never told you that I love you."

He tilts his head, eyes hooded with something close to affection. "Haven't you, though? The gentle touches, the way you colored on me, making sure I got used to your touch?" He brushes my hair behind my ear. "How you broke down every fucking wall I've ever built? You may not have said you love me, but you showed me."

"Yeah, well," I say, my knees weak from his words, his intoxicating scent, the gentle touches. "That is not the case now."

He smirks. "Are you trying to convince me of that or yourself?"

I'm so hot and flustered, I feel irritated. Irritated with how he can read me, how easy it would be to let him back in. But no. He hurt me terribly bad, I'm not forgiving him. Not this time. "I have things I need to do, so if you'll excuse me."

"It's only a matter of time. You might as well accept it, baby girl."

Not this time.

"Why are we looking for apartments?" Amiyah asks, sipping an iced coffee.

"Because I'm not living with him. I don't know if you

noticed, but he broke me. Like, really broke me. I've never felt replaceable to Vance, but when he divorced me and got engaged so easily as if we had never been, I felt like dirt under his boots. And I refuse to forgive him for that."

"No, love. I understand. But you own a home, kick his ass out. You don't have to forgive him, but he will be in your life forever. The Misfits are a tight-knit group, not to mention my godchild in your tummy. I guess I have to ask, can you watch him love someone else, watch him have children with another woman?"

My stomach sours. I can admit to myself that I can't picture my life without him. "Yes, I can. I hope he finds love, Amiyah. Just not with me."

"You're a terrible liar, Prim. He'll never let you go. We both know that."

After I drop Amiyah off, the apartment search abandoned, but shopping trip in full swing, I realize that I could live at The Misfits' home—but I don't want to disturb their lives. I make it home, carrying my bags. This child already has way too many clothes, he'll never get to wear all of them. Adriano meets me at the door and takes the heavy bags from me. "Thanks." I smile gratefully.

"Not too much longer and he'll be here, huh?"

I nod. "Yeah, it's getting a little snug in my stomach, I can't wait to get him out." I pause as my nose wrinkles, the smell making me sick to my stomach. "Oh, Adriano, what is that smell?"

He grimaces when he sees the look on my face. "I believe it's dinner."

I shake my head. "Not for me."

I cover my mouth and nose. Vance walks around the corner into the living room, frowning. "What's wrong?"

"I don't think she likes the smell," Adriano says, and Vance snaps his eyes to his cousin.

"I wasn't fucking asking you."

"It's the smell," I blurt out, trying to take the heat off Adriano.

Vance nods, grabbing his keys. "Let's go out and eat somewhere else then." I nod, following him back out of the house.

He opens the door, helping me inside and buckling me up, his hand lingering on my bump a little too long. Breaking walls down with every touch.

"Are you okay?" Vance asks after dinner, pulling into a baby furniture store.

I grimace as another hard kick to my ribs lands. "Yeah, he's just so strong." We both look down at my stomach and watch as it contorts with our son's movements.

Vance's eyes widen. "Holy shit."

"Yeah, the doctor says he's a big baby. She wouldn't be surprised if he comes a little early. By the way he's measuring, she thinks a C-section is a huge possibility." I push on what I believe is my son's butt and it bumps my hand back. I giggle before sobering. "What are we doing here, Vance?"

"We need to buy furniture for the nursery." He looks up at me. "Primrose, I don't want you to live somewhere else with our child. I want you both with me so I can protect you. I want to raise him like we're a real family. I know what I did was rash, and you don't understand, but I can't let either of you go. I won't. After the baby is here, if you still want to leave you can, but I need to protect you both. So, please, Angel. Just for now, agree you'll stay with me."

"We'll stay," he smiles, "but this is not a relationship, Vance. I just want my son to know his father and it makes sense we live with you." And after everything, we do need his protection. And I'll do anything to protect my son.

"The house is yours, Primrose. I'm living with you."

I sigh, opening the door. "Let's go pick out furniture."

"Why is this crib a circle?" Vance asks, narrowing his eyes at it as if it's a puzzle, which makes me smile.

"They're coming back in style," I supply, my hand skating over the wood.

He shakes his head. "I don't like this one."

"Don't like it, or can't build it?"

He grunts, "I can build anything."

"No worries, I don't like this one either. I like the black iron one over there." I point to the antique-looking baby crib. It's all black and I think it'll go with our gothic mansion.

He nods. "So do I, and look, matching furniture." He walks over to the display room of blacks and whites. Different patterns making up the scheme. You could do anything with it. "Do you like the entire showcase?" he asks.

"I really love all of it. You could do anything with it. It's not a standard jungle room or anything like that."

"Ma'am," he calls the sales lady over. "I'll take this," he points to the showroom.

The sales lady smiles, "Lovely crib, sir. I'll ring it up."

Vance shakes his head. "No, I want the entire showroom. Every piece."

"Every piece?" she stammers.

He looks over to me, rolling his eyes in that way that gives away his pedigree. "Yes. And while you ring that up, I'll continue shopping." He walks away.

I smile at the lady. "Don't take it personally, he's rude to everyone. I apologize on behalf of his manners." I pat her shoulder before following Vance.

"This car seat turns into a fucking stroller. What do you think?"

"Are you even looking at the prices?" I know he's not.

"Why would I do that? I can buy this entire store and still buy ten vacation homes."

"Vance..."

He picks the box for the car seat up, carrying it over to the register. "My son only gets the best."

I sigh, following him around the store as he buys things I'm not sure we will even need. We're both new to this. We have no clue what we're doing.

Neither one of us.

30
VANCE

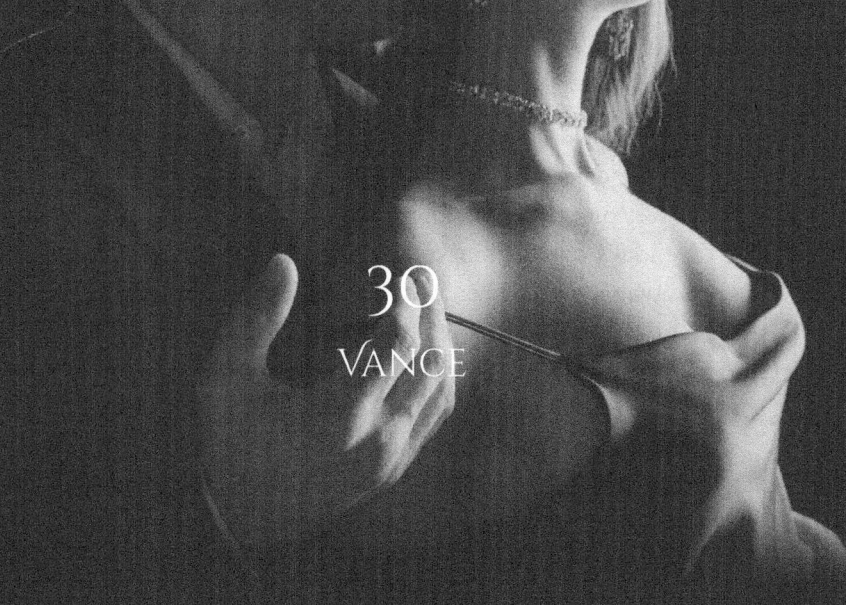

I watch as Beckett finishes the last details of the storm I had him paint on the wall. I could have done it, but I knew that sappy fuck wanted to help. "What do you think?" He steps back, admiring his work.

"I should have hired a professional."

"Shut up, you bastard." He laughs, cleaning his space up and moving the plastic off the newly installed carpet.

In hindsight, the carpet should have been laid after the painting, but I was too excited. Madden curses low as he tries to put a changing table together. "This is impossible." He sits the Allen wrench down.

I pat my fully finished crib, smirking. "We can't all be good at everything."

Madden stands, stretching his arms as he yawns. "I'll be back tomorrow."

I laugh. "I'll finish up here, you guys go get some rest." They nod, leaving. I pull my shirt off, tossing it as I lower myself in front of the changing table, looking down at the instructions.

"Here," Primrose says, handing me a glass of water.

"Thanks, Angel," I say, taking a healthy gulp as I watch her eyes light up as she takes in the nursery. "Do you like it?"

"I love it," she whispers, tears streaming down her face.

"Then why are you crying?" I put the glass down, walking behind her and rubbing the back of her neck.

She tosses her hands up. "I don't know. It's just something I do." She wipes the tears on her cheeks, smiling. "You guys are doing great."

I catch a tear against her scarred cheek and her eyes close. "Why don't you go sit in the glider and keep me company while I finish up?"

She nods. "Okay, just let me go grab the baby blanket I'm working on."

Primrose leaves and returns with a big deal of yarn and crotchet needles in a range of sizes. She sits in the glider, Samson jumping in her lap and curling around her stomach as she works. "I don't think you've ever been as beautiful as you are carrying my child."

She pauses, cheeks heating. "I'm a whale."

"Nah, baby girl." I'm quiet as I work, but then I ask, "How long before you took the wedding ring off?"

She swallows. "I kept it on until you announced your engagement. I thought you were coming back for me until then."

My chest constricts at her words. I look down at my hand, my black wedding band still resting there as it had since she slipped it on. Maybe I should tell her the truth. That the papers she signed that day were the deeds for the house. I hired lawyers to pretend the divorce was final. I needed her to hate me, forget about me until I eliminated the threat to her. I needed eyes on another so they would leave my angel alone while I found them. She would have learned we never really got a divorce if she ever tried to get married again. I didn't plan to be away from her forever, though.

I wasn't lying to my father when I said it was her or no one.

I clear my throat. "What did you do with it?"

She nibbles on her bottom lip. "It's in my jewelry box."

I nod. She kept it, which means I still have a chance. I allow her to work as I do, finishing the changing table a couple of hours later. I look over and find her asleep in the glider, arms folded over her bump with a sleeping cat at her feet. I walk over, kissing her forehead and shutting off the light.

SMALL HANDS SHAKE ME AWAKE. I SIT UP QUICKLY, FLIPPING ON the lamp to reveal Primrose crying. "What's wrong?"

"I had a bad dream. I saw the white mask and..." She shakes with her impending sob.

"Come here," I say, scooting over and lifting the blanket. She crawls in beside me, resting her wet face on my bare chest. I run my hands through her hair. "I'm going to find and kill them. I promise, Angel."

She nods into my chest. "I know you will."

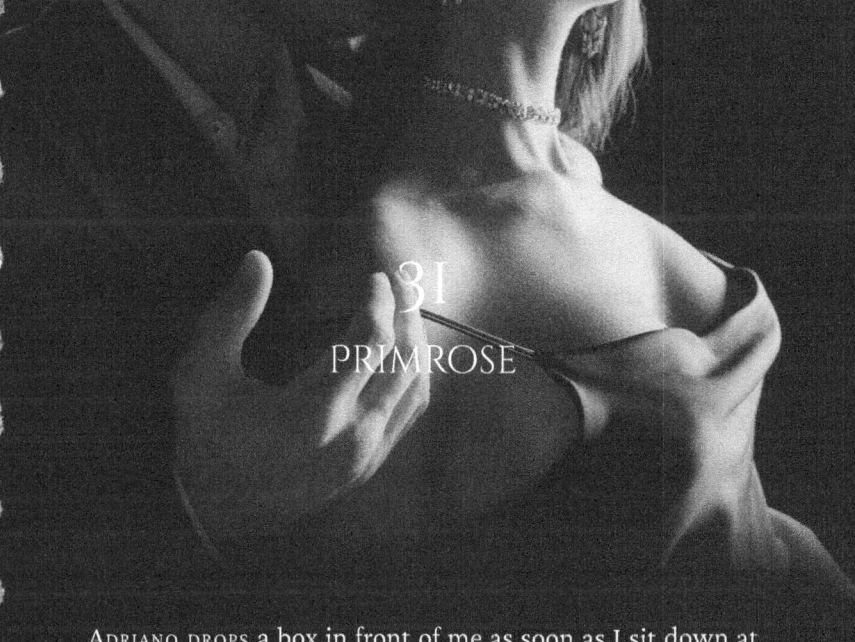

31
PRIMROSE

Adriano drops a box in front of me as soon as I sit down at the table when I get home after my classes. "Package came in for you today."

I look at the package, no return address. I frown, taking the knife from Adriano and cutting the tape. I sit the knife down, slowly pulling back the flaps. Baby blue tissue paper greets me, and my lips pull into a smile. It's just a baby present, probably from Amiyah. I laugh, shaking my head as I pull the tissues back.

A scream gets caught in my throat as a dismembered baby kitten lays in the box. A note that reads, *Your baby is next.*

The scream finally breaks free, and Adriano grabs the box quickly, peering inside and letting out a low curse.

"What the fuck is going on?" Vance asks, white dress shirt sleeves rolled up, blood staining his hands.

Adriano hands him the box and Vance's jaw hardens. "Where did you get this?" he asks Adriano.

"It was laying by the gate."

Vance watches him, pulling out his phone. "Send

twenty soldiers to my house." He pockets his phone. "You don't leave this house until this is delt with," he says to me.

"What about my baby appointments?"

Vance sighs, rubbing the bridge of his nose. "Adriano or I will take you, but you need to listen to me when I say, you don't leave this house anymore."

"Okay," I whisper.

Vance gives Adriano the box. "Get rid of this." And then he looks down at his hands. "Fuck, let me go get cleaned up."

I stand, wiping my cheeks. "What were you doing?"

His eyes harden before he responds. "Torturing people for information."

"Can I... can I see?"

He tilts his head. "Why?"

"If I'm going to be in your world, I would like to see what I'm bringing my child into."

He sighs. "Come on, Angel."

Vance leads me into the woods. The sky is gray and purple, thunder rolling in the distance. We stop at an old shed. Vance punches in a code and looks over his shoulder. "It's not too late to turn around."

I shake my head. "I want to know."

He pushes the door open and nods for me to walk in first. I come to a halt. The shed looks old on the outside but the inside has been renovated. A man hangs from the ceiling, half of the white mask he wears is melted to his face as his body is split down the middle, exposing his insides. I hear Vance washing his hands behind me, but I don't turn to look. Solely focused on one of my attackers.

"Where did you find him?" I ask.

"He was staking out the house. Caught him trying to climb over the fence."

I nod. Not sure what to say. If this place isn't safe, nowhere is. Vance walks up behind me, moving my hair to one side of my shoulder. "Every one of them who hurt you will meet this fate." He kisses the back of my neck. "Does this scare you, Angel?"

I shake my head. "No," I whisper.

Vance's fingers tangle with mine, pulling me away from the body. We walk out into the storm. Vance slamming the door behind us before he grabs my hand again. We make our way out of the woods, the rain heavier in the open space. "Wait." I say, stopping and looking up at the sky, watching the tiny drops grow fatter as they splatter on my face.

"What are you doing?" he asks.

"Enjoying the rain, isn't it beautiful?"

VANCE

"Enjoying the rain, isn't it beautiful?" she asks, a smile somehow appearing on her face after what I just showed her.

I don't give a fuck about the rain, but the woman embracing the storm takes my breath away. The way she stood before her attacker, brave and relived at the sight of his mutilated body, never blinking an eye. How she told me she wasn't scared, not of this life and not of me. "Fuck this," I say, stepping into her personal space.

My hands cup her neck, tipping her head back as I slant

my lips over hers. She gasps into my mouth, tiny hands resting on the soaked material covering my chest. I've waited months for this moment. To feel her body pressed against mine, her mouth on mine. I don't fucking deserve it, but I'm too selfish to not take. All I do to this woman is take, but I can't stop. I want to own everything of hers. Even if it's her heartbreak. Because she's mine.

I coax her mouth open, marveling at her taste. Wrapping my arms around her waist, I lower us to our knees in the wet ground as rain pounds down on my back. I gently lay her on the ground. Her eyes glaze over in lust as she looks up at me, pulling on my shirt so I lower over her. Her hands, gentle as ever, unbuckle my belt, moving my pants down as she wraps a small fist around my cock. I groan into her mouth, sucking her tongue into my own. I reach under her dress, pulling her panties from her body, and she guides me into her warm, silk heat. She moans, head tipped to the wet earth as her back arches off the ground. Her hands roam up my back as I thrust into her. "Wife," I murmur into her hot, panting mouth. Elated I'm not a freak and can finally find peace in her touch.

"Not anymore," she moans, nails digging into my back.

I bite her bottom lip, pulling on it as my hands trap hers above her head. "Do you hate me, Angel?" I thrust, making her cry out.

"Not in this moment."

I chuckle, burying my face in her neck. "Still my filthy little slut, baby girl?" I whisper next to her ear.

"Always," she whimpers, her pussy spasming around me, her body shuddering as she holds on to me.

I come with her, my body hardening as I release ropes of cum deep inside her. "That's good, baby," I say, pushing her wet hair out of her face, bending and laying a kiss to her swollen belly.

I love you, Primrose.

I think it, but I don't say it. No matter how badly I want to.

32
PRIMROSE

A HAND RUBBING my stomach wakes me. I look down to see the big, tattooed hand, wedding band shining off the sunlight. I noticed he still has it on, but if I ask about it, it may give him false hope. That this is more than us having sex and raising a child together. *Which sounds crazy, even in my own head.* I shake the thought away, locking up my heart.

These end-of-the-last-trimester hormones are killing me. Anytime I see him, I pounce. Which is why I wake up every morning in his arms, but that's all it is. I still haven't forgiven him. My lady parts have, but my heart hasn't. Storm kicks against his dad's hand. I know I said I would wait to see his face, but the name Storm just feels right.

"You two could have let me sleep in." I yawn, pressing my face into my pillow.

"He already has my temper. He's been trying to move my hand off you all morning." Vance chuckles, which makes me smile.

"Let's hope not," I say, about to rise, but Vance flips me over.

He grabs my left hand, placing my wedding and engagement bands back on my ring finger. "I need to tell you something," he says. I stare at the rings, throat clogging up. "Look at me, Angel." I do, eyes ready to spill over with unshed tears.

"I lied. We never got a divorce. I needed you to believe we did so you'd give up on me. I had to protect you, and the only way I knew how was to separate us. I needed you to hate me. Because I knew if you didn't, you would have never given up on me."

I let out a shaky breath. "I signed the papers. I met with the lawyers in their office."

"You signed deeds and the lawyers were for show. That was really just them finalizing the house and finances."

I shake my head. "Why would you hurt me so deeply like that, Vance? I don't understand."

"To protect you," he says, cupping my cheek.

"To protect me you had to hurt me?" He's silent. "Why not just tell me your plan?"

"Because I needed the world to believe I was done with you. Take the attention off of you while I figured out who was after us."

"Is this the part where I'm supposed to forgive you?" I ask, smacking his hand away. I want to punch his stupidly handsome face.

"No, it's the part where you get angry, yell at me, and then admit you love me."

My chin quivers and I rise. "I have an appointment to go to."

"Let me take you," he pleads.

"No, I need space to digest this." I lean over, kissing his cheek. "We'll talk when I get back."

"Angel."

I sigh, shutting the bathroom door and leaning against it. Letting the tears fall.

Adriano drives, humming to the song on the radio I'm not paying attention to. I'm too busy watching the sideview mirror. "Hey, Adriano. That car has been following us for a while now."

Adriano looks in the rearview mirror just as our tires pop. "Fuck," he says, pulling over. The black car follows, and I begin to panic when men in suits and white masks step out.

"Adriano," I whisper and look over.

"I'm sorry, Primrose," Adriano says, reaching under and pulling the white crying face mask from under his seat. He places it on and then jerks me by my hair to him. I struggle as he places a white cloth over my nose and mouth. I try jerking away, try to escape. It's useless as my car door flies open and my eyes close.

Last time I was in this position, I basically gave up. I didn't have anyone to fight for, but this time, I have my son. I look around the same cell. The same metal bars and concrete floor. I don't flinch as the cell door swings open. The same smiling mask as last time. Her heels echo as she walks closer. "So, we meet again."

She drops to her haunches in front of me. Her hand coming out to touch my stomach. I send my foot into her stomach. She grunts, falling back. "Someone tie her legs up. Now," she barks, dusting the dirt from her pristine white pantsuit. "And here I thought we were becoming close friends."

"Son, come," she says to the dark space in the corner of the cell. The crying face mask walks from the corner, holding something sharp and shiny. Two other soldiers come forward, restraining my legs using the chains.

I watch as the happy face masked woman takes off her mask. Lucia smiles at me. "Surprise."

Everything in my body sinks. It's been her the entire time. Vance had no chance of tricking her into thinking he was with someone else. She had an inside spy, and he didn't even know it. *Adriano*.

Adriano takes off his mask, face void of anything. Looking anywhere but at me. "Bring him in."

Two soldiers in white masks carry in Vance. He's hands are bound, and his eyes widen when he sees me. His movements become desperate as he tries to escape their hold on him. Screaming something through the cloth in his mouth. "Just tie him up, but close to her so he can watch this time. Last time didn't seem to be effective enough." They pull Vance next to me, chaining him up close, but not close enough to touch. "Remove the cloth from his mouth, I want him to scream," Lucia orders.

They rip the cloth out of his mouth and Vance looks to me, checking over every inch of me as he asks, "Are you okay?" I nod in response.

"Lucia, why are you doing this?" he spits.

She raises an eyebrow, turning to look at me. "I know she told you. Question is, why didn't you listen?"

"I get threats on a daily, none are ever effective."

Lucia shrugs. "True, but I am about to be very effective.

I'm leaving you no choice. I'm going to make you watch as I kill everything that matters to you before I take your life. Oh, my brother will be sad, but he'll probably blame the Russians. And Adriano will finally get his rightful spot." She waves Adriano over. "Now, show Momma you deserve all she does for you. Cut the baby out."

"No," I gasp, pulling on the chains, trying to break free.

"Let her go, just kill me. I'm the one you want gone. They have nothing to do with this," Vance says.

"Remember when you were fourteen and put a gun to my head? Told me our love was nothing special? Well, I used to have a heart and you broke it that day. Now, I'm going to break yours."

Adriano pauses, face contorted in disgust. "Wait, what?" he asks.

"No need to worry about it now. Go on, cut the bastard child out."

Adriano swallows, clutching the scalpel tighter in his hand as his eyes shine when they meet mine. "Adriano," I shake my head. "Please, don't do this."

He looks away, taking a step back. "Weak," Lucia sneers, grabbing the scalpel and handing the tool to another guard. "You, cut the baby out."

He nods, stepping up to me. "I'm going to kill every one of you when I get out of these chains. Do not lay a single finger on my wife," Vance growls, pulling the chains hard enough the brick wall they're attached to cracks.

Lucia laughs. "Special nephew, you will not get the chance."

The guard positions the scalpel low on my stomach and I fight with all my strength to free myself. "Just fucking kill me, Lucia," Vance yells.

I scream as the scalpel sinks into my skin. The pain is

worse than the hot metal that sizzled into my face when I took a bullet for Brixley, worse than the pain of watching my mother die or any whip my father ever laid on me. The pain isn't only physical, but emotional. This baby is mine, a part of me. The only good thing I've ever been able to call mine, and now they're taking it away from me.

I grit my teeth to keep from begging—I won't beg. But I do scream, tears streaming down my face as I squeeze my eyes closed, shutting Vance's screams out of my mind. The scalpel disappears and I open my eyes to see Adriano has knocked the guy out. Lucia's face is murderous as she points the gun at her son from behind him. "Adriano, duck!" I cry. He drops down as the bullet sails past him and into Vance's shoulder. The bullet rocks him back, knocking his body into the wall.

"Vance," I cry, watching Adriano slide something over to him.

"Adriano, get her out of here, now." I see Vance working the locks with the key Adriano gave him. Adriano grabs the scalpel, sending it flying through the air and piercing his mother, before he sends a bullet into her thigh. Dropping in front of me, he lets a tear slip as he presses on my bleeding stomach.

"Come on, Primrose. I need to get you to a hospital." Adriano picks me up, and I hold on to him desperately as I watch Vance take another bullet, this time to the chest, causing him to sink into the wall.

"No," I cry, trying to get out of Adriano's grip. "We can't leave him."

"I'm sorry." Adriano sniffs. "He told me the day he took me in that if it comes to him or you, to save you."

I scream as I watch Lucia walk and stand over Vance, gun raised at his head. My world stops, and I can't breathe.

I'm hyperventilating as I hold my hand out to reach for Vance. And then he's gone.

"You have to push, Primrose. Come on, sweetheart," Vance's mom says, holding on to my hand on the left side. The trauma and stress caused my water to break, and I didn't even realize it due to all the blood. I shake my head, laying my head against Amiyah's chest, who sits behind me. *Where he is supposed to be.*

"I can't do this, not without him," I cry.

Brixley squeezes my other hand. "You will, Primrose De Luca. This baby is the only thing that matters right now. You are the only one who can do this. Now, sit up and push. You think Vance would want this?" I sob, sitting up and grunting as I push again. "There you go, Prim," Brixley praises.

"All right, Primrose. One more push and he'll be here."

I look to Brixley. "Oh god, what if I'm a bad mom?"

"Little late for that. Come one, Prim. Deep breath. Do it with me." I take a deep breath with Brixley and as I release, I push with everything in me.

The wail of a baby makes me smile, tears rolling down my face as I stare up at Amiyah. She looks down, eyes shining as she bends to kiss my forehead. "He would be so proud of you."

My heart breaks a little more and I don't stop the sobs that rack my body as Amiyah holds me close.

"Come on, now," Amiyah says. "Let's see that masterpiece you created."

She helps me up just as a perfect baby is placed in my

arms wrapped in a white, blue, and pink blanket. A full head of coal black hair and soft tan skin. The smallest little nose, with those lips Brixley and Vance share. "He looks like my son." Vance's mother sniffs, wrapping her arm around me.

Storm opens his blue eyes, taking us all in. "Welcome to the world, Storm. This is your family." I pull him close to my face, nuzzling him.

33
PRIMROSE

My body feels as if it's wrapped in a warm cocoon. But I know it's a false fantasy, because I know he's gone. Storm and I have been home for a little over five hours now. My friends wanted to be with me, even though they stayed the three days me and Storm were in the hospital. Storm had to remain in the nursery for twelve hours so that the doctors could monitor his breathing, but they have concluded that he is perfect.

I knew coming home was something I needed to do alone. To come back to our home where I shared so much with Vance.

Love, hate, trust, and now, sadness.

After I got Storm settled in his room, I came to our room and broke down at the sight of his side of the bed, still unmade. I laid in his spot, soaking up his scent that's embedded into his pillow. Wrapped the blanket around me as if he was holding me, and I lost it again. I finally got up and pulled one of Vance's t-shirts out. Bringing it to my nose and inhaling it, I collapsed back on the bed, curling into a ball as I tossed and turned into a fitful night's sleep.

My mind wakens to the sound of something on Storm's monitor. I quickly sit up, running into Storm's room, and pause at the sight of the dark figure in the rocker holding my son. The figure looks up and says, "Looks like we woke Mommy up." At the sound of his voice, my knees buckle, and I drop to the floor.

"Vance?" I croak.

"Miss me, Angel?"

I begin to cry, crawling toward them and resting at his feet. "You wish," I say brokenly.

VANCE

Once I get my son back to sleep, I pick my limp wife off the floor, carrying her to our bedroom. Her hands cup my face, laying gentle kisses all over it. I drop us into the bed, and she sits on my lap, pulling up my shirt. "Where is your gunshot scar?"

I raise my shirt up, showing her my shoulder. She frowns, shaking her head. "I saw you get shot in the chest."

"I had a bulletproof vest on."

She stares at me, lip trembling as she glares. "Why didn't you say something? I thought you were fucking dead." She hits my shoulder. She only uses that language when she's really upset. I'll just have to add it to the list of things I need to apologize for.

I capture her wrist. "Calm down. I had something I had to do before I could come to you. No one told me you went into labor until after."

"My God, I hate you, Vance De Luca."

I lean up, capturing her lips in mine.

"A simple phone call would have worked," she says, breaking away from my kiss. "I mean, seriously, Vance. Do you know how scared and sad I was?"

"I'm sorry."

She pauses. "What?"

"I'm sorry. For breaking your heart, for making you and everyone else believe I was dead. I'm sorry for everything, Angel." I cup her cheek. "Well, I'm not sorry I fell in love with you or that I forced you to marry me. I'm not sorry for the beautiful child we made together—" She cuts me off, laying her lips over mine.

"I love you, Vance," she whispers into my lips.

"I know," I say just as Storm begins wailing from the room across from us.

Primrose pauses, smiling and laying another kiss to my lips before crawling off the bed. She walks across the hallway and I lay my head on my pillow, grunting at my broken ribs when I shift.

"Storm wants to sleep with us," my wife says from the doorframe, holding my son in her arms as she peers down at him with tired eyes that hold so much love it makes my chest explode.

She climbs onto the bed, resting her body into mine. I peer down into wide blue eyes that match his mother's. He yawns, tiny hands curling into fists as he tries to seek out his mother's chest. Primrose begins nursing him, rubbing his small forehead with her thumb. "Is it wrong to be a little jealous?" I ask.

Primrose laughs, rolling her eyes. "I'm sure you'll get your chance in six to eight weeks."

"Weeks?" I ask, an eyebrow raised.

She nods. "That's how long it takes to heal."

"Speaking of healing, how is your stomach, did he cut you deep?"

She shakes her head. "No, it only took two stitches. Adriano stopped him in time. But what about you, honey?" She looks over to me, tears clinging to her lashes. "How did you make it out? The last thing I saw was a gun pointed at your head."

"As soon as they took you from Adriano's car, he called me. Told me what was happening. I guess he grew a conscious. Anyways, he told me they were coming for me. Before they got there, I called my father for backup. I should have died, but Lucia's gun jammed right as my father's men busted in."

She nods. "Okay, and what did you have to do before you came home?"

I run my tongue over my teeth, wondering how she is going to take this. "I got honored in as the head of the De Luca crime family. I officially take the leader role in two months."

She's silent, digesting the news, I presume. "Okay. And what about Adriano?"

I scoff. "I'm ninety percent sure he was one of the men who raped you, Angel. I have him held up with his sick mother."

"But he saved us."

"I don't fucking care. He touched you, hurt you, spied on us. He is a traitor, and traitors die."

"Show this one mercy."

I shake my head. "This isn't up for discussion."

Primrose rises, laying a sleeping Storm in the bassinet next to her side of the bed. She turns to me before saying, "I don't think he raped me. He knocked me out, so I'm not certain, but I don't think he did."

"He's still a traitor, Angel."

"He's our family."

I'll never understand the gentle nature of this woman. Of how she can be so forgiving. I love her for it, but fuck, I can't let him live. "Let's talk about it in the morning."

She nods, climbing into bed and snuggling in my arms. I kiss her forehead, tightening my arms around her. "Goodnight, Angel."

"Goodnight, honey," she whispers. And I smile.

34
VANCE

"There is my grandson, come to Papa." My dad ignores me completely, snatching Storm from my hands.

"Nice to see you too, Dad." I usher Primrose inside.

"You're not important anymore, son. I'd get used to it." He smiles down at Storm but pauses as he hears my mom basically running down the stairs. "Come on, grandson. Let's go hide before your meme decides she's going to steal you from me." My dad ducks into the den with Storm in his arms.

I have to hide my laugh as my mom emerges, hands on her hips. "He is hiding with him, isn't he?"

"Afraid so." I smile.

"No worries, I'll find them." Mom kisses Primrose on the cheek, taking the diaper bag off of her. "Date night, huh?"

"Something like that," I murmur.

"Well, you two have fun, don't hurry back. Just go on vacation if you want." And then she's gone.

Primrose laughs. "We may need to watch them, they're

the type of grandparents to take our son on vacation and not tell us until they get there."

"I have eyes on them, no need to worry."

She laughs again, taking my hand as we go back to the car. "Where are we going?"

"You'll see," I say as I open the car door for her, helping her in.

WE WALK INTO ONE OF MY FAMILY'S HOUSES OF TORTURE. IT'S AN old warehouse out in the middle of nowhere. Windows have been shot out for fun, the floors a dual rustic color—and no, it wasn't designed that way. This is where people come to never be seen again. Two of my soldiers sit at a card table, guns close by as they play dominos. Usually, that would piss me off, but Lucia is not going anywhere.

Primrose stops as we get close to the iron chair. Lucia's eyes are closed, and if you didn't know any better, you'd think it was some old chair she's sat on. This one, however, has iron spikes that hit every point of the body. It's painful but not entirely deadly. The spikes only break skin, nothing too deep. They don't even make you bleed since the iron spikes plug the wounds. That's until we remove her from the chair, but even then, I have something else planned for her.

Primrose tilts her head as she examines Lucia. "Is she alive?"

"Not for long." I motion the guards to pull her up. They do, causing Lucia to scream as blood begins leaking from her body.

"What even is that?" Her question holds more intrigue than disgust.

"Iron chair," I reply, nodding my head at the soldiers. "I like medieval torture devices. Fascinated with them, really."

The guard hauls Lucia onto the Spanish donkey—the tringle-shaped wood. I think after what she did to me, to my wife, this one punishment is fitting. Lucia turns her head, bloody body on full display. "Vance, please, I'm your aunt."

I smirk. "Add the weights, she doesn't have long but I want her to feel this."

The soldiers add weights to each of her feet. Lucia screams as the board slowly rips her up at her crotch. The weights stack, the screams turning into pleads of God and mercy. But like everyone before her, she splits, silencing her cries and taking her miserable life with her. I turn to Primrose, but she's no longer beside me.

"Boss, what do you want us to do with her?"

"Burn her, let wild animals eat her. I honestly don't care." I walk outside to find Primrose leaning against the car. "You okay?" I ask, walking up to her.

She shakes her head. "That was too much for me."

I kiss her forehead. "Okay, Angel. No more torture scenes for you."

"Can we go?" she asks.

"I've got to deal with Adriano first."

She places her hand on my bicep. "Can I at least talk to him first?"

I grit my teeth. "Yeah, come on."

Adriano is chained to a wall in another room of the warehouse. He lifts his weak head, holding eye contact as we near him. Primrose leans down in front of him and asks gently, "Did you rape me?"

Adriano shakes his head. "I couldn't do it. I couldn't even watch like the rest. I hid in my car until it was over. Doesn't mean Vance shouldn't execute me. I did nothing to stop it either."

Damn right. Adriano is a weak bastard, just like my father said. We have no use for someone like him.

"And why did you save us? Why the change of heart?" she asks, emotion in her voice. She'll never admit it, but I think she was fond of him.

Adriano looks down, throat working. "Because I care about you, Primrose. How could I not? I watched after you day by day. Watched you conquer your demons, watched as you were passionate and considerate about everyone around you, even me. I couldn't let my mother hurt you or your baby."

Primrose nods, walking over to the wall and grabbing the keys. And then she fucking uncuffs him. "This is me repaying you for saving my son. But I never want to see you again, Adriano," she says, stepping beside me.

"We never agreed to this," I say close to her ear.

"I'm your wife, which makes me just as much in charge."

I smirk, wrapping my arm around her shoulders. "Count your blessings, Adriano, because if I ever see you again, I'll gut you, and my wife won't be able to save your miserable excuse of a life then."

We walk out of the building, and I open her door. "Where do you want to eat?" I ask.

She makes a face. "Nowhere, Vance. Did we not just watch the same thing? I'm good."

I chuckle. "Come on, baby girl. A little violence is good for the appetite."

She shakes her head. "Let's do something else instead."

"I've got an idea."

"WHY ARE WE AT THE ABANDONED DORMS?" PRIMROSE ASKS.

"Here." I hand her the bandana. "You'll need this."

She takes it, tying it over her mouth, and looks over to me. "Are we hunting the new recruits."

I shake my head slowly. "No."

She pauses, eyes watching me. She lets out a giggle and then takes off toward the worn-down dorm. I smirk, grabbing my duct tape. I tie my bandana over my mouth, twirling the duct tape around my finger as I walk to the dormitory, whistling.

I enter the run-down lobby, pausing to see if I can hear any sounds, but she's oddly good at hiding. I creep up the stairs, jumping over the rotting holes and coming to the top floor. "Angel," I call out, but no answer comes. I check the busted doors, looking in the stairwell. Nothing. I go in the old shower rooms; the room would be dark if it wasn't for the missing roof, the moon my only light.

I catch something move to my right and snatch my wife by

her long blonde hair. "Got you," I rasp, using my grip on her hair to make her bend to her knees. I pull her arms back, taping them so they're pinned behind her back. "Wish you picked dinner?" I ask, stopping in front of her, unbuckling my pants.

She licks her lips, eyes peeking up under dark lashes. I grip her hair, running my tip over her lips before thrusting deep down her throat. She chokes, eyes shining as she wraps her skilled tongue down my length. I pull back out, groaning as I sink back in. "I'm—"

I'm cut off by my phone and growl as I answer it. "What?" I snap.

A throat clears. "Sir, it seems your parents are trying to escape with the baby. I don't think it's serious but..."

"Of fucking course they are." I click the phone off, pulling Primrose to her feet. As much as I want to fuck my wife's face, I have to go stop my parents. Because they could disappear with my son, even if it's only to Florida for a week, but still. Boundaries are important and taking our son without permission is not fucking okay. I can't help but laugh a little at the situation.

"Kidnapping grandparents?" Primrose asks as I cut the tape from her arms.

"Yep, come on, Angel." She giggles as I pull her to the car with me. If her giggling is the last sound I ever hear, I'll die happy.

No one told me marriage was hard. You sacrifice as much as you give. You have to work at it until your dying breath. But I'd burn the world to the ground for my wife. Laying the ashes at her feet, all while making sure she never gets burned in the process.

There was ever only one love for me. And she's wrapped in so much light it's blinding.

But she is my forever.

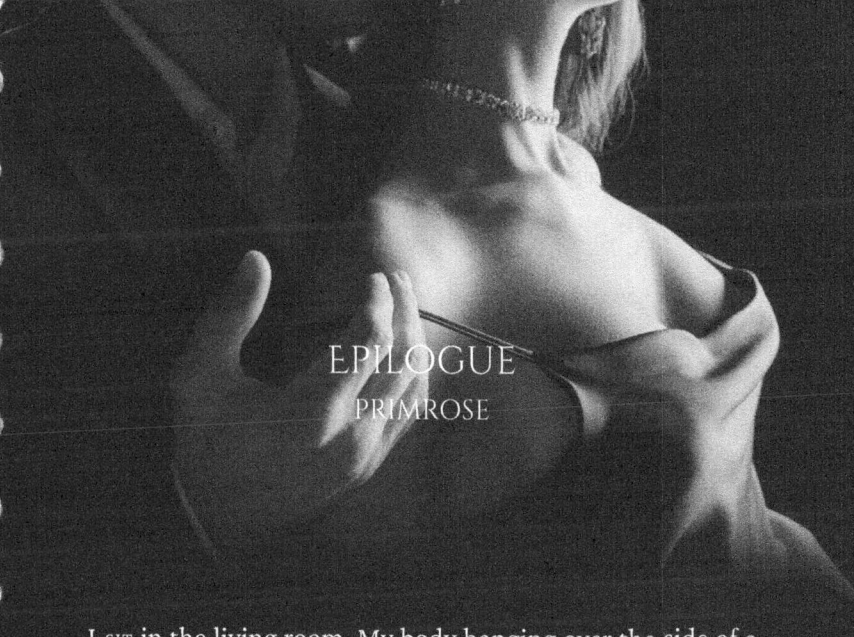

EPILOGUE
PRIMROSE

I sit in the living room. My body hanging over the side of a chair as I read another outlaw romance. It's my thing, don't judge. I'm waiting for my ruthless husband to come downstairs so we can go on another honeymoon. It's our ten-year anniversary this week. His parents are keeping our children. Our nine-year-old, Storm. Our triplets, who are eight. Because we are crazy and thought more kids was what we needed. Lorenzo, Aurelio, and Nicolo. Printer copies of their father. Swear on everything. And last—I swear it's my last—Rain. My blonde-haired, dark-eyed five-year-old. My only girl. I dropped them off earlier. They were ecstatic to get away from us. It seems the older they get, the less cool we are.

"Did you drop the hellhounds off?" Vance asks, stepping into the living room.

He's aged so beautifully. Like fine wine. His face has gotten sterner, but I love that about him. His rough, jagged edges are what have always drawn me to him.

I wrinkle my rose, frowning. "You can't call them that. They're angels."

He laughs. "My sweet baby Rain is but those other four are no angels. The triplets broke my favorite golf clubs."

I bite my lip to keep from smiling. "I told you not to let them use those clubs."

"And Storm? He may look like both of us, but he's me. There is something so dark about him." Vance shakes his head.

"Well, I love dark things, so..." I shrug.

I don't have a favorite child, but Storm and I connect a little more than the rest of my children. They are close with their father, but Storm is truly all mine. And if he's a little dark, who cares.

"Fuck, Angel. When did we get old?" He pulls me up, kissing my lips. "We got hella kids in this house."

I laugh, kissing his scar. "But isn't it a beautiful life?"

He smiles. "It is. All thanks to you." I blush as he grabs my hands. "You have everything you need for our honeymoon?"

"Yep, all packed," I nod.

"You ready to be my dirty little slut?" he rasps.

I blush, sighing as I lean into him. "Always."

THE END

Afterword

Keep reading for a sneak peek at Reckless Conduct. A forbidden, age gap, teacher/student romance.

CALLUM

JOURNAL ENTRY: SOMETIMES, YOUR INNER FREAK AWAKENS IN INAPPROPRIATE PLACES.

Freedom, the power or right to act, speak, or think how one wants. To not be enslaved to another.

I never truly thought about what freedom means. Sure, I've written essays on it, but never for my own thoughts. I've written about what freedom in this country means. I mean, we all have. But have I truly thought about what freedom means to me? No. No, I haven't. Because I've never had mine taken away.

But as I sit here in my car, staring at my high school on my first last day of school, the word is like a neon sign in my head, lighting up over and over again.

Freedom. Is there truly such a thing? We're enslaved to our jobs, our grades. Enslaved to the expectations of our family. A hostage to money, to the bills we must pay. Even those with no responsibilities are slaves to something as well. The people who backpack across the country are enslaved to weather conditions. Homeless people are enslaved to the basic need to eat. As people, we are all enslaved to something. I could go on, like how addicts are victims to their addictions, or street children are vassals to surviving, but I have personally never seen any of that. I'm quite sheltered from the struggles of day-to-day life.

When I walk across the stage in May, diploma tight in my grip, hat soaring through the crowd as we cheer, my first right of freedom is granted. But I can't help the feeling that maybe it's a trap.

A knock on my window has my eyes jerking from the orange-red brick building to the sound. Jake, sweet, caring, loving Jake, presses his forehead to my window, sandy brown hair wet and curling from his recent shower. Brown eyes, a deep melted chocolate. Plush lips tipped into a smile, forcing his two identical dimples to poke out of his cheeks. Jake's aura is addictive, like a euphoric warmth that spreads over your body. He himself is contagious.

And my boyfriend.

I smile, pressing the button to lower my window. Jake pokes his head through, a gasp parting my lips as he bends down and kisses me. Pulling back, his fingers tug on my bow. "You ready for today? Last first day of high school."

I smile, pulling down the visor and flipping the mirror open, my hands carefully placing the bow back into place. "As ready as I'll ever be, I suppose." The truth is, I'm not ready. Jake, as amazing as he is, is a morning person. I, however, am not. Catch me any other time of the day and I'm basically Strawberry from *Strawberry Shortcake*, happy with a smile always planted on my face. But mornings? They always feel like a red flag.

I grab my lipstick, a red to complement my red-and-navy-blue plaid skirt, and apply it carefully. Red stains like a bitch, and the chances of fully getting it off my skin is highly unlikely. So, I must apply it carefully. My shirt is white, a pearl button at the top to bring the colors together. My style is preppy, I love dressing up. I would make fashion my whole personality if I could.

I flip the visor up, grabbing my leather backpack and my coffee. My hands twitch to put my headphones in, to avoid all things *morning*, but Jake and his charming smile and dimples, holding my door open for me, has me caving, taking a deep breath in order to conquer the world.

As soon as my heels hit the payment, Jake throws his arm around me, pulling me flush to his side. "I can't believe we're almost done with this place. Free from the controlling world of high school and parents."

It's on the tip of my tongue to ask if he's ever thought about what freedom actually means, but instead I say, "I don't know, my mom's pretty chill. And I don't hate our school."

There are classmates leaning up against cars most dream to own, but unfortunately, never will. Some of them being obnoxiously loud for seven-thirty in the morning.

"Really?" Jake muses. "I kind of wish my parents put me in public school, private school is so basic, uncultured." He grimaces as a cup of coffee flies right in front of us, barely missing me.

"Yeah, but at least we don't have to wear uniforms like most private schools." Which I'm so grateful for. Imagine not being able to reflect yourself through your style? Gross.

"Which is a crime. Plaid skirts? Stockings? Sounds like a good time to me."

I smack his stomach lightly, his hands capturing mine before I can pull them back. He brings them to his mouth, biting my thumb, and why does that... make my stomach all warm and fuzzy? Do I maybe want to be bit? I don't know.

CALLUM

Jake and I, we've only kissed so far, a little foreplay, but maybe I'm ready for more.

We enter the big glass doors, a buzzing energy in the air. High ceilings, marble floor a deep brown color with light swirls of cream through it. The lockers are a deep clover green. It smells the same as it has for the past three years. A light scent of bleach mixed with pencil shavings and old dusty books. I set my bag in the crate, using my student badge to scan myself in, then the guard gives me the luxury of walking through the scanner. Preston Boyd Preparatory School is high on security. One of the safest schools in the state. The guard nods at me, telling me I'm free to get my things and get the hell out of the way. I grab my things, stepping to the side to wait on Jake, who grins as he grabs his belongings, walking over to lace his fingers with mine.

People greet us, waving and asking about summer. I'm not usually rude but I can't find it in me to pretend I'm happy to be socializing this early in the morning. Finally, we stop across from my first class of the day, math. Jake wraps his arms around my shoulder, bringing our noses flush as he leans us into the wall. "Want me to come over after school?" he asks.

I brush a strand of hair off his forehead, rubbing my nose against his. "Yeah, I'd love that."

He grins, eyes going over my shoulder, watching something. "I got to go, but I'll see you in government." He kisses my cheek, walking past me to high five Josh, the caption of the baseball team. A dreamy sigh leaves my lips, but I'm being interrupted by the bell.

I walk in, choosing the desk in the corner for the year as Mrs. Williams walks in, all bright smiles and clapping hands like being here is the best thing ever. "Okay, mathematicians, it's never too early for some college equations!"

It is, in fact, too early for all of this, Mrs. Williams.

Today hasn't been bad. Not spectacular or anything, but definitely not bad. Except for maybe lunch. Sitting with Jennifer, Veronica, and Macy is mind-numbing. I love celebrity gossip as much as the next girl, but not the part where they judge without having all the facts. My friends—and trust me, I use that term lightly—are kind of bitches. They're cruel and opinionated. We have nothing in common except for being pretty. And for some reason, that means we must be friends. Social norms suck.

I'm on my way to government—kill me now. It's not that I think government is not important, I know it is, but I despise all things government. I won't lie, the hype about the new teacher does bring me a certain level of curiosity.

I walk through the door, my heels halting, my heart... is it beating? I'm not sure, because right in front of me is the most desirable man I've ever seen.

His tall, imposing frame, so much like *his*, takes up most of the space behind the podium. His raven hair is almost like *his*. And then he turns to look at me, ashwood eyes narrowing, not like his, but just as beautiful. The stubble on his strong jaw is mesmerizing, coupled with his thick eyebrows. The high arch of his cheekbones, made for the front of magazines, not for teaching high schoolers. His arms, thick ropes of muscle as he crosses them over his built chest. *Is it hot in here?* He clears his throat, and thankfully my brain is there to help me out to send signals to my feet to move or I would have stood in the doorway all day, staring at him.

The bell rings as I get to the table where Jake sits, grinning as he pulls my seat out for me. I sit, thanking my boyfriend before turning to face the front of the class. His black pants are tight, accentuating his ass as he turns around and starts writing on the dry-erase board.

His voice is rough gravel that wraps around me like smoke when he speaks. "My name is Mr. Boyd and I'll be your government and economics teacher this year."

I knew I was sick.

Twisted and tormented.

When I find myself wanting an older man—my teacher, to be exact—that's when I realize my daddy issues are very much real.

I figured out fast that my family wasn't normal. And not just because they gave me what would be considered a boy's name in every country except in Scotland.

No, I figured it out when I saw *him*. In the newspaper, front and center. Governor Collins. With his family. Except, Mom and I were not there.

See, I always believed the man who gave me life was always away because he was the state governor. It makes sense. After years and years of seeing him with *them* in the newspaper, smiling, linking his arms with his wife, who was beautiful with her chestnut hair, small button nose, and model-like body. She sadly died two years ago. Fatal gunshot at a peaceful protest. Most people in my position would have been ecstatic. I, however, was not. I mourned the loss of my brothers' mother. My brothers, all tall and imposing like him. With raven hair and sharp jawlines. One's eyes, the oldest, is blue like mine. Taking after our father. While the other two favored the brown of their late mother's eyes. Mom and I... we're his other family. The one he keeps under lock and key. The one who lives at the very opposite end of the city. Farthest away from him and his true family.

I don't know why I didn't notice it sooner.

How I have to always refer to him as Richard instead of Dad. How he always brushes me off in favor of holding my mother.

He loves her.

Truly loves her.

And I think he may love me, too, but not enough to allow me any perks of having a real father.

When he arrives, it's with a present. Expensive and shiny.

With small "Go play" and "No hugging."

I figured I was probably a mistake.

He wanted my mom.

Not me.

He wanted to have his perfect family and his true love on the side. He wanted one family and since I didn't come with a penis, I was of no use to him.

So yeah, not normal.

My mom told me he was just busy and to give him time to come around. To be thankful for my lavish life and the best education money could buy.

That I should be lucky he didn't give us a settlement and sweep us under the rug.

And I am—I am thankful for my life. It's cozy. Rich.

And I want for nothing, except...

I want acceptance and love, but he couldn't give it to me. No matter how hard I tried. How amazing my grades were. How beautiful I turned out to be.

I wasn't good enough.

Not for *him*.

When I asked if I could meet my brothers, he shut me down. Said to never call them that because they never were or will be my brothers.

So yeah, not normal.

So, it's really no wonder that this man in front of me has my heart clashing against my chest, thighs clenched tight, desire seeping from between my legs every time I see him.

He is the next best thing to sooth my raw heart. To fill those dark, tormented spaces...

So yeah, sick, twisted, tormented daddy issues.

My earlier thoughts of freedom flashes in my mind. And it should scare me.

Because I know, if given the chance, I'd give up all my freedom and be enslaved to Mr. Boyd.

Jake and I sit on the floor in my room. The carpet is a cream color, pairing so beautifully with the pink and bright white accents in my room. We both sit against the foot of my bed, backs resting into the white fur comforter. I'm sorting my binders out, writing names on folders for school. Matching syllabuses to the correct classes instead of having them in a jumble mess in the one folder I stuffed them all in today.

Jake's finger traces up my inner thigh, causing me to stop working on my organization to look over to him. His brown eyes sparkle as his head moves closer to me, finger lightly brushing the hem of my skirt. His hair brushes across my forehead, nose gently pressed to mine, lips barely a breath away. "You seem stressed, Callum. Let me help you with that," he whispers over my lips.

I lick my lips, nodding. His mouth brushes mine. Once, twice. His hand slides along my inner thigh. Higher until it slips inside the silk of my panties, connecting with my wet heat. It's not that Jake doesn't turn me on, because, God, he does. Especially when he kisses me. It's gentle and sweet. He does this thing with his tongue that always has me gasping and pulling him closer.

He pushes another finger inside me, coaxing a moan to slip past my lips. His lips leaving mine, causing my eyes to pop open. "I want to try something different. Are you okay with that?" he speaks across my mouth.

"Yes," I whisper.

He smiles, planting a soft kiss to my lips before shifting down, gently spreading my thighs and settling between them. I close my eyes, a mixture of excitement and embarrassment tinting my cheeks. His fingers hook into my panties, tugging the scrap of silk down my legs, pulling until they clear my feet, tossing them over his shoulder. He looks down at me, and this time, I can feel the redness of my cheeks spread over my entire body. He looks as nervous as I feel but when his head bends, tongue tentatively swiping over my sex, the feeling so intense and new, I almost lose it. I almost push him away, but then he does it again and again, until his tongue works my tight hole. A moan breaking free. Embarrassingly loud. And when he doesn't move from the spot, avoiding the spot that aches, I begin to get frustrated. He is trying, his tongue sloppy and missing that bundle of nerves that is so sensitive, I long for it to be licked, rubbed. Devoured. But he keeps missing it, choosing to thrust his tongue in and out.

I want to get off so bad, I can taste it.

Gripping his soft strands in my fingers, I jerk his head up to look at me. "Touch my clit, Jake. Please."

CALLUM

His brow furrows, face slightly confused. But as he gets back to work, he finally finds it. But something is off. I squeeze my eyes closed in frustration. Men could be... But then it happens. My mind conjures him up. Putting me on his desk, the classroom empty except for the two of us. His ash eyes watching me as he swipes his tongue over my clit, tasting me. Devouring me. Savoring every last drop. His eyes are heated, dilated with lust and hunger. His strong, manly fingers bite into my thighs, pulling me closer to his mouth. I feel it then. The curl of my toes, the heat that blooms on my insides, the need to grind myself against his face as I rise to my ecstasy. I feel the release jerking my body, whimpers leaving my mouth as I thrust myself harder against his stubbled face. Soaking my legs. My chest heaves and my eyes flicker open. My ceiling coming into view, the glass chandelier swaying just a bit. "Wow," Jake whispers, and I look up at him, my cheeks heating in embarrassment. "I don't think you've ever come that hard before."

I want the world to open up and swallow me whole. I gulp, forcing a smile to my face. "Yeah." What else can I say? Because Jake didn't get me off, if it was up to him, he'd still be working his hardest with no success.

Jake didn't get me off.

No, thoughts of Mr. Boyd did.

ACKNOWLEDGEMENT

To my friends and family, of course. I wouldn't be here without you. Your love and support means the absolute world to me.

To my little team. Camille, Amanda, Kira, Danielle, Nichole, and Keeana. I love you girls so much. Thank you for your love and support. I've grown very attached to each and every one of you. Thank you for taking a chance in me! And more importantly, thank you for being my safe space.

To my beta readers Tiffany and Aundi, thank you so much for your feedback as well as your love and support!

To my husband, I love you so much. Thank you for your support!

To my little monsters, I hope you're watching me making my dreams come true and know deep in your heart you CAN do absolutely anything you set your mind too. Here's to hoping momma can provide you with the life you truly deserve.

To Mel. I freaking love you. I have absolutely no idea what

ACKNOWLEDGEMENT

I would do without you. You are my right hand and soulmate.
To Sarah and Tanaka, I would be so lost without both of you. Thank you for always taking care of me.
To Rumi, I adore you so much. You will never truly know how grateful I am to have you.
To my readers, again, still so shocked I have any, but you guys are truly amazing. I hope I can grow close to every single one of you. You are SO important to me; words cannot even describe. To the readers, bloggers, and influencers who signed up, reviewed, and can promoted We Vow in Sin. I'm forever in debt to you. Thank you so much for the love and support.
If you have a second, please consider leaving a review!
XOXO, MT

About the Author

MT lives in Texas with her husband and two children. She enjoys reading a good fantasy/PNR romance as well as a good cup of coffee. She has old lady tendencies even though she's in her mid-twenties. And writing her own bio is very cringe worthy to her.

M.T. Morgan tends to bounce around the romance genre. She may make you laugh, cry and cringe. It just depends on her mood.

Email MT: authormtmorgan@gmail.com
www.authormtmorgan.com

Also by M.T. Morgan

STANDALONES

FABRICATED

RECKLESS CONDUCT

SINNERS' PLAYGROUND

WE DANCE IN SIN

WE VOW IN SIN

WE LAY IN SIN (coming soon)

Made in the USA
Coppell, TX
02 March 2026

72711729R00144

PRIMROSE THATCHER HAS SPENT HER ENTIRE LIFE IN A CAGE.
ALWAYS LOOKING THROUGH GOLDEN BARS
UNTIL SHE CAN FINALLY ESCAPE.

COLLEGE IS BLISS, HER ONLY FORM OF FREEDOM,
FILLED WITH DANGEROUS GAMES
AND THRILLING ADVENTURES SHE FINDS JOY IN.
BUT WHEN HER MOTHER BECOMES SICK,
SHE'S FORCED BACK IN HER GILDED CAGE ONCE MORE.
HER MOTHER'S DEATH CAUSES
HER TO SHIFT FROM ONE CAGE TO ANOTHER. HIS CAGE.

VANCE DE LUCA.
RUTHLESS MAFIA HEIR. THE DEVIL.
AND MY NEW HUSBAND.

THEY SAY BETTER THE DEVIL YOU KNOW,
BUT IT TURNS OUT…
SHE NEVER TRULY KNEW HERS. UNTIL NOW.